DIRTY REBOUND

A Slayers Hockey Novel

MIRA LYN KELLY

Copyright © 2020 by Mira Lyn Kelly

DIRTY REBOUND

Photographer: WANDER AGUIAR PHOTOGRAPHY LLC

Cover Designer: Najla Qamber, Najla Qamber Designs

Editor: Jennifer Miller

For Lisa Kuhne

Chapter 1

Cammy

"*L*ook, Cammy, you're a nice girl. Easy on the eyes. And I tried to give it a chance," he says around a yawn he doesn't bother covering. "You know, gotta respect the single mom and all. But I'm just not feeling it."

Gah, me either.

Zipping my parka against the biting January night air outside Wagner Arena, I nod as fans stream out around us. "I understand."

I *understand* that I should have held out longer with the hockey tickets. Stretched it another month, maybe even two. But he was persistent, *whiny*, and fine, I felt guilty about using him. Even knowing he was using me for my connections to the Slayers hockey team.

Why did I think this was a good idea?

I'm a romantic. And despite a pretty rotten track record when it comes to guys—present company included, thank you—I still believe in happily ever afters.

This guy was no candidate.

He does that neck-twitch thing that drives me nuts and winces. "You gonna be okay getting home on your own?"

Seriously? I blow out a steamed breath and force a polite smile. "I'm fine."

Sympathy shines in his eyes and I kind of want to puke a little. "Keep your chin up."

"BULLSHIT!" George snaps from across our table in the back of the Five Hole. "If you're going to break up with someone, you do it *before* the game. Not after. Never after. Is he here tonight?" Straightening in her seat, she scowls toward the front end of the bar. "I bet he's here."

"He is." I huff, picking at the damp label on my beer. "A couple friends were waiting for him when he finished dumping me. It was super awkward walking fifteen feet behind them all the way from the arena to the bar."

2

"This is why I avoided dating hockey fans," Natalie groans, absently rolling the fat diamond on her finger. "It's so hard to read when they're really into you instead of being into your brother—or brother-in-law in your case." Her brows furrow. "No wait—Julia had that thing so Greg donated his tickets tonight. George and I sat in Vaughn's. Whose seats were you in?"

"Rux's."

Pinching her lips together against a laugh, she shakes her head. "Oh man, he's going to be pissed."

"So pissed," George gleefully agrees, clinking her beer with each of ours.

Six more bottles land on the table as Quinn O'Brian leans in between them. "Hey Georgeous, who's gonna be pissed?"

The girls are out of their seats in a flash, George throwing her arms around Quinn's neck, and Natalie giggling as Vaughn Vassar sweeps her into his. It takes another minute before Rux clears the crowd. He's tall and broad, dressed in one of his gorgeous custom post-game suits, chestnut hair combed back, but it's that cocky smile that sets him apart. This guy. Even as he drops into the seat beside me, fans are still slapping his back.

Slinging a powerful arm around me, he flashes a huge grin. "You see it?"

"Nice breakaway." It was beautiful. Tie game with

thirty-seven seconds left in the third, and he scored the winning goal.

Pulling me in tight, he presses a quick kiss into my hair and then leans back, looking around. "Where's what's-his-name?"

"You mean The Blip?" George offers, getting comfy in her man's lap. "Probably jerking it to a selfie from your seats."

These girls are the best.

Rux leans back with a satisfied smile. "You finally drop his ass?"

I choke on a swallow of beer.

This time Nat is the one chiming in. "Not exactly."

No more smile.

Between the music and the amped-up post-win crowd, the Five Hole is pretty loud, but I swear I can hear his molars grinding together as she fills him in. Rux has been a little overprotective of me since I scored what Natalie calls surrogate-little-sister status, but I think of more as being besties-in-law. And the look on his face right now is about as threatening as I've ever seen. But I'm pretty sure I don't have to remind him of the no-beating-up-Cammy's-ex-boyfriends rule.

"*Keep your chin up.*" he growls. "Is he fucking kidding?"

I lean into his side for a squeeze. "I know, right?

4

Like I'm going to be so broken up about losing *him*? Please. And honestly, I can't even be angry about him waiting until after the game—because, come on, Slayers tickets."

Everyone around the table grudgingly agrees.

"The thing that rubs is I only agreed to go out with him because he asked like two hours after I found out Jeremy was moving back to Chicago. And I didn't want to be single when he got here. But now, not even a month later and here I am… single again."

Rux shakes his head. "What do you care if Jeremy thinks you're dating someone? That asshole left you pregnant at eighteen."

I shouldn't care. After all these years I wish I didn't. But the way he left me was brutal.

"I guess I just wanted him to see that I'm doing fine without him." That I'm not waiting anymore.

"Sunshine, you're better than fine. So you don't date much—"

"I'm *choosy*." Careful. Patient. God, have I been patient.

"Hell, yeah you are. And you're also an awesome, hot-as-fuck mom with an incredible kid, a sister who would lay down her life for you, and kickass friends who love you. Plus, you're rocking a great job that lets you work from home, your fridge always has the best snacks, and you score Slayers tickets on demand. Babe, you're killing it."

I feel myself getting a little misty, so I focus on the fun. "Your seats are pretty great."

I grew up on football thanks to Julia, but since she married into hockey, I've seen the light.

"Right?" Reaching for my other shoulder, Rux pulls me around so we're facing each other and I'm looking into his dark brown eyes. So it's just him and me. "Jeremy know *who* you were dating?"

"No." He hasn't even asked.

Which is totally fine. It's not like I thought Jeremy Levenson would be banging my door down trying to score some long-overdue second chance. He's had seven years and hasn't done it yet. Besides, if he's really back for our son, then I don't want anything else muddying the waters.

A nod. Rux looks past me. His eyes get hard, and I swear the next breath he takes fills his chest to twice its size, broadening his already intimidating shoulders. Following his glacial stare, I find The Blip standing a few feet off, his fangirl eyes locked on Rux.

"Yo, Rux, great game tonight… buy you a beer?"

No. Freaking. Way.

I turn back to Rux, expecting the seams of his suit to be busting open. But instead of going full-on Hulk… he's smiling. Sort of. This isn't Rux's real smile, the one so contagious my son can't see it without breaking into fits of giggles. This is something else. Something dangerous.

Rux nods to the guy I'm pretty sure he wants to take apart. "Yo, thanks for getting out of my way."

Out of his way? What's he—

In the next second, his mouth slants over mine in a kiss so unexpected, that in a million years I wouldn't have seen it coming. A kiss that startles me still, frozen in his hold as he bows me back through one heartbeat, two… *thirteen*. When Rux pulls clear, he looks past me to where The Blip is standing red-faced and open-mouthed, and growls, "*Leave.*"

There's no argument.

The table is silent around us and I still haven't blinked.

George breaks the silence, eyes wide, and whisper-squeals, "Rux is your dirty rebound!"

Finally, I sputter, "Rux, you just kissed me!"

He winks. "You're welcome."

Rux

"RUXTON MEYERS, YOU ARE *SO DEAD*." Blue eyes the color of the summer sky narrow to slivers of pure wrath as my bestie glares up at me. I'm thinking it's kind of adorable, but then she balls her fist, planting it on her hip, and I realize this is serious.

"Whoa, you're *pissed*." She is. I've seen it before, just rarely directed at me.

"Um, *yeah*?" She looks around the deserted back hall, blonde curls bouncing around her face. "What were you expecting with that kind of stunt? *You kissed me!*"

At the risk of making things worse, I shrug and own it. "Seriously, I was expecting more of a *thank-you*."

Definitely not Cammy Wesley grabbing me by the ear and towing me into the back hall of the Five Hole so she could jab her pointy finger into my chest until I'm pretty sure I'll have a bigger bruise from her than from getting racked into the boards in tonight's game.

For a second, she just blinks up at me—then her face scrunches up and she jabs me again. And even beneath the bar's dim lighting, I can see her cheeks turning pink. Wait, red.

Oh shit.

She's never going to let me into her fridge again. Matty's going to grow up playing football instead of hockey. What have I done?

"You said you wanted Jeremy to think you were seeing someone," I start, scrambling for my defense.

"And then that little waffle stomper was headed over and I figured—two birds, one stone. Set The Blip straight on who needs to keep his fucking chin up and start some rumors circulating about who you're seeing."

With Greg Baxter out, the last few games have been rough. People are watching, waiting to see what happens. And pulling out that last-minute save tonight is going to have eyes on me.

This place is crawling with snap-happy fans and probably some press too. Someone caught that kiss and, guaranteed, by tomorrow everyone's going to know about it.

Problem solved.

She throws up her hands. "And how am I not going to look desperate—no, scratch that—how am I not going to look totally pathetic when a week from now The Blip sees you with your tongue down some bunny's throat?"

I hold my finger up and she cocks her head like I better make this good.

"First, when was the last time you caught me with my tongue down anyone's throat?"

I've been on a bunny break for a while actually.

Her arms cross. Slowly. "Um, it was in this very bar, actually. Against that wall."

Okay, and I know what she's talking about,

because when I'd come up for air and saw her across the bar—it didn't feel good. So it was the last time. "That was months ago."

She rolls her eyes. But I'm right.

"And secondly, who gives a shit what that guy thinks?"

"I don't. Not really." She loses some of her steam and her shoulders droop. "But... don't you have any exes who have said stuff about you that you'd like to prove wrong instead of right?"

The question catches me off guard and, shoving my hands in the pockets of my suit pants, I clear my throat. "Look, you know I'm not really cut out for the kids-and-white-picket-fence life. Relationships aren't my thing. But of the *very* few women I've dated seriously… they pretty much hit the nail on the head."

"What did they say?"

"I'm impulsive. Irresponsible. Unreliable and all over the place." To start. The rest… I don't want to go there.

Cammy looks like she wants to argue. She's sweet like that, always seeing the good.

But we've got this honesty thing going, so I don't sugarcoat it. "They're right."

After a breath, she shakes her head. "Well, I don't know about that, but—"

"But you don't want The Blip to be right about

you," I supply. For as much of a trooper as Cammy is, handling anything life throws her way and never backing down, my girl is vulnerable too.

"It doesn't matter," she mutters.

The hell it doesn't.

"Cammy, look at me." Those big blue eyes come up to meet mine. I can't stand the idea that she's upset and would pretty much slither on my belly over broken glass to take that worried look off her face. "Hey, I'm sorry. I just wanted you to feel better."

I want to protect her from the guys who don't deserve her.

Hell, I want to protect her from everything. It's been like that for three years. Since that first night I went over to her place with Greg to pick up Julia. There was Cammy. Twenty-two years old, Matty clinging to her side. She was so happy for Julia, smiling that bright, beautiful smile while we took her sister out and she stayed home. I could see the longing in her eyes, the envy. Only the second she looked down at that little boy, it was gone.

She was such a good mom. Trying so hard.

At first, I just wanted to help her out. Give her a break once in a while. So I'd make sucker bets with Julia, offering up babysitting here and there. Cammy'd come home and we'd talk a little about her night before I left. The next time we talked a little more.

And pretty soon it wasn't just babysitting and it wasn't just about wanting to help her out. We fell into the kind of easy friendship you don't find with most people.

She shakes her head and lets out one of those long breaths that usually mean she's getting over her mad. "I know. And thank you." The corners of her mouth tip, and it's like the sun coming out after a month of rain. "Did you see his face?"

"The Blip's? Hell yeah, I did. Pretty sure his mouth hit the floor hard enough to rattle his teeth."

"Rux?"

"Sunshine."

She rolls her eyes, but I know she likes it when I call her that. And it fits who she is perfectly.

"No bunnies next week."

I get another little jab in my chest for good measure, and then catch her finger in my hand and pull her in for a hug that feels like everything good in the world. "Not a problem."

Chapter 2

Cammy

"Come on, you've got to tell me," Julia begs the next morning, her arms stretched across the kitchen table in a plea as pitiful as I've ever seen my sister deliver.

I'd planned on getting a few hours in on my medical coding job before Matty came home, but once she heard about that kiss, there was no putting her off —not that I'd want to. Julia and I talk about everything and I miss having her around like crazy.

But thank God for flexible hours.

"Was it good? Gross? Did he, like, try to eat your face or was it one of those tight-lipped Afterschool Special kisses? Rux is such a showy guy, I'm betting it was one of those kisses where your lips are closed but you move your face all around."

I ought to answer. After all the years of living vicariously through Julia's love life, demanding details only a little sister would dare to demand, it would be fair. But dang it, she never gave up the goods without making me work for it at least a little, and turnabout is fair play.

So I pretend to read over the field trip form in front of me. Move my pen down the page—I'll have to read it for real later, they might need a chaperone—and blink innocently across the table we used to share.

Her eyes narrow. This girl gets pro athletes to spill their tea every day—she's a woman to contend with. But she's also my sister, and in a battle of wills, I'm not going down easy. It would be an insult to the both of us.

Finally, she cracks. "Cammy!"

And who am I to keep her in suspense? "Okay! Okay, okay, okay. Relax. I'll tell you."

She props herself on her elbows, her fingers drumming the table impatiently.

I lean in. "It was fine."

"Fine?" she coughs, rocking back.

"I know, it would be so much more fun if it swung further to one extreme or the other, but the truth is, as kisses go, Rux's was neither here nor there."

"Tongue?"

"Come on."

"Well, I don't know. Open mouth or closed?"

"A little open. He kind of caught me mid gasp. I didn't see it coming and then"—I fling my hands up, Kermit-style—"there it was!"

Julia makes one of those sort of noncommittal noises and I nod.

"See what I mean? It's not like he had BO or a saliva problem."

"No, Rux always smells good," she says, picking at the peel of a Halo orange like she's trying to make confetti.

"He really does." Reaching across the table, I smack her hands away, peel that sucker in one strip, and hand it back.

She's impressed. And rightly so. But the awe over a Halo peel has a shelf life of maybe three seconds and Julia is still looking at me. Or maybe watching me would be more accurate.

"What?"

Her head angles to the other side. "*Rux.*"

"No." I know where she's going and just *no*. She keeps watching, and I heave an impatient breath. "Julia, I know it would be all kinds of adorable if I ended up with your hubby's wingman, but as much as

I love Rux"—and I absolutely do—"we exist solely in the friend zone."

"Mmm."

"Seriously?"

She gives me one of those nearly imperceptible shrugs she mastered back in high school and waits. So apparently, yes. Seriously.

"Fine. I'll break it down for you. Rux is incredible. He's loyal and funny. Good looking. And he might love me almost as much as he loves my kid."

"Rux is the best."

"I know, right?" I sigh at how lucky I am to have him in my life.

"And maybe someday he'll get it into his head for five seconds that married life might be fun—and ten seconds later, he'll make some bunny a very lucky WAG. But not me."

"He's successful, fun-loving, emotionally available, into your kid, and come on with the 'good-looking' business. He's *hot*. Not like Greg, but if you like them just a little wild."

"Yeah, see, right there. That's the issue. I don't want wild. I want *stable*. Reliable."

Julia levels me with one of her no-BS looks. "You don't want wild?"

Dang it, she knows what she's doing. And now I'm thinking about what everything *wild* might encompass and I feel a bit warm. "Not for anything more than a date with Bob." Who doesn't like a good fantasy now and then?

She snorts, rolling her eyes. *"Bob*, your battery-operated boyfriend? You have to stop calling those dates, Cammy. It makes me sad."

It might make me sad too if I let myself think about it too much, but I don't. What I think about are all the ways I'm so incredibly lucky in my life. With Matty. My sister. Rux, who definitely falls under the *little bit wild* heading—which is why he's so much better as a friend.

"Whatever. All I'm saying is that wild is fine for fantasies. But it's not what I'm looking for long-term." And we both know, long-term is, ultimately, what I'm after. My very own happily ever after. "I want a nice guy. A guy who's in it for the long haul, someone Matty and I can count on… I want a guy who's maybe a little bit *tired*."

"What?" she laughs, shaking her head.

"I'm not interested in a guy who's going to have temptation thrown in his face every other hour for the rest of his career—whether it's another team, a more beautiful woman, or just the next adventure. I want the guy who's *already had the adventure* and maybe just likes the idea of staying home."

"Staying home? You get out like once every other

week." She looks around, eyeing the apartment we used to live in together. "These are some cushy digs, but Cammy, seriously, haven't you had your fill of staying home?"

I wave her off. "Fine, staying home *sometimes*. You know what I mean. Yes, I want to fall in love and be swept off my feet. I want that heart-pounding, whole-body need to get closer… to have more." I bite my lip and rest my head in my hand. "But above all that, I want the guy who's going to fall in love with being a part of our family. So while *wild* sounds like some toe-curling fun… I'm after the happily ever after that gives Matty the kind of stability and security you and I never had growing up with Mom and her parade of deadbeats."

Julia groans, shaking her head. "Bill."

"Tim."

"Sal."

"Eww, Sal."

Our eyes meet and together we say, "*Harry!*"

Julia flattens her hand over the tabletop and takes a breath. "Cammy, we could go on listing Mom's shitty boyfriends one after the next, straight through till morning. But those *guys* weren't the real problem."

"I know." It's a quiet concession. Nothing new, but still never easy to say out loud.

Our mother was so caught up in the drama of her

love life, in her cycle of bad decisions, and whatever jerk she'd sacrifice anything not to lose, she had nothing left for us. If it weren't for Julia—I don't even want to think about what would have happened to me.

I don't want that for my son.

"Cammy, you've already given Matty all the things we never had. You put him first in every choice you make. You love him with everything you are. And more than that, you've given him a network of family and friends he can count on. That little boy has stability and security in spades."

And I never want him to lose it. Especially not because I fall for a guy—no matter how amazing he might be—who doesn't want the same things I do.

My phone pings and I smile. "Matty says they'll be home in about ten minutes."

My sister sits back. "*They'll* be home, huh? Is that what you're hoping for with Jeremy, now that he's back? After his adventure… maybe a little *tired?*"

"What, no! No way. Absolutely not. Nuh-uh. Not even a little bit."

When I'm done, she cocks her head. "How's he looking these days, anyway?"

Jeremy was eighteen the last time my sister saw him. A kid. Since then he's been married, he's been divorced, and he's traveled the world.

"He looks like… Jeremy. But like a grown-up Jeremy." It's been seven years.

Her shoulders sag, and her mouth twists into this dissatisfied little frown.

I reach for my tea. "What did you want me to say?"

"I don't know, I guess I was just hoping the guy would've lost all his hair or gotten plugs. Bad ones. Grown some benign but inoperable hump on his back."

Clicking my tongue, I smile. "You're sweet to want that for me."

"I want the best for you." Her voice drops to a whisper. "And the best would mean that Jeremy had an outside that matched his rotten, selfish inside."

There have been times I would have agreed with that assessment of the man who promised me forever and then left me pregnant and alone. Times I would have called him every name in the book. Almost as many times as I cried myself to sleep imagining what it would be like to have him come back. To me. To us.

But now that he *is* back—for Matty—I don't really know what to think.

"Well unfortunately, or maybe fortunately—I don't even know—he looks pretty much the same as always. Handsome in that kind of understated way. Fit, but obviously nothing like Rux or Greg. His hair is still thick and blond. Nose still straight. Eyes still—"

"Whoa! That's enough of that." Julia levels me with a no-nonsense look. "When you describe that guy, I want to throw up. Because I can hear in your voice the same blind adoration that was there back in high school. And this guy hasn't earned it. If I ask you what he looks like? You can tell me 'he looks okay.' That's it. And if you find yourself thinking about how thick his hair is, think about somebody whose hair is thicker." She starts snapping her fingers. "Quick, give me a name. Who has thick hair?"

"*Rux* has good thick hair." Not that I think of him that way. But his hair is actually pretty spectacular. It's this warm brown with a bit of red that comes out in the sun. Long around his face. Always looks like he just rolled out of bed. But in a good way. A little wild.

The grin is back. "That's what I'm talking about. So how's Jeremy looking these days?"

I roll my eyes *hard* but give her what she's after. "He's okay."

"Still pretty fit?"

Cripes. "I guess." And then, because she's my sister and teasing is one of our love languages, I fan my face with my hand, making my eyes as wide as they can go. "But not like Rux. Because *that guy* has it going on." I throw in a sigh. "Well over six feet tall, solid packed muscle on a frame that doesn't quit. And his face? Hard cut and just a little rough around the edges… *yummy*. But the best thing about him?"

Julia's hands are clasped under her chin, her eyes shining with delight. "Spill it."

There's a knock at the door and I stand, pausing only to say, "He's not any more interested in me than I am in him."

A minute later my little guy is flying through the front door and into my arms. He's all smiles and gushy breathless chatter about his night with his dad. I get another tight squeeze and it feels like I can breathe again.

When I look up to the doorway where Jeremy's standing like he's not quite sure he should come in, I realize that for all the things I've thought and hoped and wished about this man… the one I feel the most deeply is gratitude for giving me this boy.

Which is why I tell him, "You should probably run. Julia's here."

Rux

"HEY, MAN, COME ON IN," Greg Baxter says, wiping the sweat from his brow with the back of his arm as I step off the elevator into his living room.

He's got a sweet pad, benefits of having gone to school with Jack Hastings, the guy who owns the building. I'd give my left nut to live in a place like this—okay maybe the right nut, no, the left. I give the sac a lift. *Screw this place, you boys are keepers.*

He's currently pedaling like a beast, going nowhere on the stationary bike recently moved into his living room. If it were me, I'd have the thing facing the picture window overlooking the river and city beyond, but for as good as Greg and I get on, we're cut from a different cloth. He's got the thing aimed at his TV, where he's watching his wife's weekly show.

"Should have told me you were going for a ride, I'da brought my bike too." I can just see the reporters camped outside waiting for a bite on Slayers captain, Greg Baxter, watching me tote some giant-ass stationary bike in through the lobby.

Be better than the nothing they've got to report on his status now.

Greg flips me off, laughing as his legs come to a stop and he takes a swig from the water bottle in the holder.

It's good to see the guy smiling. With the end of my career staring me in the face, not sure I could.

"How's the shoulder?"

"About where it's supposed to be according to the docs."

That's good news, I guess. It might be better if the shoulder was the only reason Greg wasn't on the ice. But while it's what the team's been sharing with the media, the bigger issue is this guy's head. After a concussion that took him out for a good chunk of last season, the blow that put him into the boards and fucked up his shoulder also fucked up his head again. It's nothing like that first concussion, but the fact that he's having problems at all has everyone questioning whether he'll be back.

But I'm guessing that's not something he wants to get into today when he starts asking about last night's game.

"Feel like it's coming together better with Vassar and O'Brian?"

I shrug, not really wanting to admit that it's not— probably the same way he's not ready to admit what's going on with his career. Or maybe it's not the same, since it would be hard as hell to look the guy I've been paired up with for the majority of my career in the eye and tell him I was rocking it without him.

And despite that miracle last night, I'm not.

Not with Vassar and O'Brian, and not with any of the other matchups Coach has been trying out either.

"Hey, it'll happen, man."

It would if he came back, but Baxter isn't just the team captain and my partner on the ice. He's my friend. And keeping him safe is more important than anything that happens in a game.

He takes another drink. Then, "How are the guys?"

"They'd be better with their captain back."

He shakes his head, pointing the nozzle end of the bottle at me. "They've got their captain. Forget what your sweater says. The only reason it's not official yet is because—"

"Because you're their captain," I cut him off. "And you will be until there's an official announcement that you're out. And we're not there yet, right?"

He nods and even though that *yet* is looming large between us, the tension in my chest starts to unwind some. I know I'm in line for the capital C, but truth? I'm not sure I'm cut out for the job like Greg is. I'm the bomb when it comes to backing him up. So assistant captain, hell yeah. But captain isn't a patch I've ever coveted. I care about the team too much to risk letting them down.

"All that bullshit aside, you oughta come out with the guys. They miss you."

"Yeah, maybe." He turns back to the big screen and takes another long swallow.

I head to his kitchen, shove my face into the fridge to see what kind of goodies he and Julia have stocked in there. I got a guy who comes and fills my fridge too, but it's never as exciting as what's in somebody else's.

"Stay the fuck away from that sandwich!" he shouts from around the corner.

Muttering a curse, I slide the grinder that looks amazing back on the shelf and close the door. Walking back into the living room annoyingly empty-handed, I drop onto the giant-ass couch.

"Dude, Cammy says you kiss for shit."

Yeah, right. "Ha-ha. Try again. What did Cammy really say?"

There's an evil glint in his eyes and it's a hell of a lot better than what's there when we're talking about the game that's been a constant through our whole lives up to now. "Said your mouth was disappointing as fuck. Took a Sharpie to the ladies' room wall at the Five Hole and dropped a one-star review."

"Bullshit." I kick my feet up on the coffee table. "No way she said I was a bad kisser. I'm the fucking best... Your mom told me so."

Greg groans, his head falling back on a laugh. "Dude, you did not."

I lick my finger and touch the air above my head, adding a little sizzle sound effect.

"But for real, man, what were you thinking kissing her?" He meets my eyes and after a moment, laughs again. "Right, you weren't."

Story of my life.

Chapter 3

Rux

"How the hell is this possible?" I bellow from Cammy's kitchen. Her fridge is always stocked. She has the best snacks. *Homemade* snacks and tons of them.

I was hungry before I left my house, but knowing I was coming over here, I waited for the good stuff. Cupcakes. Zucchini bread. Those giant chocolate chip cookies she keeps a bag of in the freezer.

But today, nothing.

"Where are the snacks?"

She steps into the doorway, notching her fist at her hip.

"Are you seriously looking for food?" she coughs out. "We are literally leaving for dinner now."

I'm always hungry. And her fridge is always stocked. I point inside.

"Where's the food?"

That patiently amused look she's giving me fades and a hint of worry edges into her eyes.

"Matty was concerned there wouldn't be anything to eat at his dad's tonight. I told him I was sure it would be fine, but he filled the beach cooler with half the kitchen anyway."

I close the fridge, my appetite gone.

Cammy is putting on a good show of letting that dick twizzler into Matty's life, but I know it's killing her every time she has to let her kid go. She could have told Jeremy to fuck himself when he showed up back in Chicago, but she didn't. Having grown up without a father herself, she wants more for her son. And because her heart is so damn big, she cares about Jeremy getting a second chance with Matty too.

Ask me, anyone who would leave their pregnant girlfriend because he couldn't handle the responsibility is a serious asshole and doesn't deserve another chance at the gift he threw away. But bad as it burns, I don't get a say. So I'm just trying to be there for my girl best I can.

She deserves it.

"Matty nervous his dad was going to try and feed

him sun-dried tomato hummus with water crackers again?" Yeah, I heard about last time.

"Seems like it," she says with a soft smile, but the worry is still there.

"That kid's all you. Smart as a whip. He wasn't sure his dad got the memo, so he decided to show him how it was done." And then even though I know she knows it, I also know it doesn't hurt to hear it, so I add, "He's gonna be fine."

She takes a breath that's a little bigger than normal and gives me a smile that's not quite as bright as usual. And I thank God she's not holding a grudge about that kiss. Because I can see in her eyes, Cammy could use a hug.

Pulling her in, I draw a deep breath of the vanilla shampoo I like so much. Her arms come around my waist and she relaxes against me.

"Thank you, Rux. I needed that."

Maybe I did too. That's the thing about being with Cammy—she gives me things I didn't even realize I needed. Things that soothe a place inside me I do my best to forget—the one it's too late to fix.

I've got a lot of shortcomings and I wouldn't wish me as a husband on my worst enemy, but when it comes to being Cammy's friend, I'm rocking it. In this, I'll never let her down.

Running a hand over her back, I peer down at the spill of blonde curls against my shirt.

"And I need food, Sunshine. What do you say we get out of here and grab some."

She laughs into my chest, and damn if that isn't the best feeling in the world.

"Yeah, let's get out of here."

I let Cammy pick the restaurant and we end up at this divey noodle joint we've been to a couple of times before. They don't take reservations and couldn't care less about me being a Slayer, so we always have to wait, packed into the alcove by the door with everyone else—but the food is totally worth it.

We eat and talk and joke. She shows me the pattern for the Lego Masters apron Matty asked her to make him. We haggle over what we're gonna watch tonight, I want *The Curse of Oak Island* and she wants *Blacklist*, which always kills me, considering how many romance novels she's got loaded on her phone. But when it comes to TV, she's all about the action and intrigue. That or rockumentaries.

Chances are good we'll watch hers, but it's fun to negotiate whose pick is first.

By the time I've polished off the Thai Basil Chicken Cammy couldn't finish and the check is paid, I'm feeling pretty good about the smile on my girl's face. We head back to the alcove, weaving through bodies to where the coats hang by the door. I help her with her coat and she wraps the blue scarf I got her for Christmas into some kind of elaborate knot while I shrug into my jacket.

Suddenly I feel her hand in mine. My eyes come up because while we're pretty touchy-feely with the hugs and me just kind of liking to be close to her, hand-holding hasn't really been our thing. But then that delicate hand delivers a crushing grip that has me wondering if I'll be able to hold my stick for tomorrow's game.

"Damn, woman, what—?"

"Do it again," she whispers through a kind of scary smile.

Do what again? I helped her with her coat. Bumped at least four people because it's a tight fit and I'm a big guy. But I *apologized*. Still, if she thinks I need to do it better—I start to turn to the guy behind me but stop when she delivers another bone-grinding squeeze.

"*What?*" Look, I'm a pretty quick guy, I don't miss a lot. It's what makes me good at what I do. Right now though? I have no idea what this woman wants from me. But based on that freaky intense stare she's giving me, whatever it is, she wants it bad.

"Kiss me. Now," she demands through teeth that don't move. "He's here!"

And it clicks. "The Blip?"

I start to turn but for being a pretty little thing, Cammy's surprisingly strong and snaps me back with a hissed, "Don't look. Don't look. Don't look."

I try to wipe the smile off my face, because, come on.

"What? You were mad when I kissed you two weeks ago. Now you want another?"

That pissy huff. "No, I do not *want* another, Ruxton. But I'd rather have it than have The Blip think you just gave me some pity kiss or worse"—her face morphs into this tragic mask of horror that has me wanting to pull her into my arms without even knowing what *worse* is—"a *pity lay.*"

Choking on a strangled laugh, I pat her hand while carefully extracting mine.

"Whoa. No one thinks that, Sunshine."

"Think about what he said to me. He thinks I'm desperate. That I have no options. He thinks I'm the kind of woman who would make easy pickins for a player like you."

"Easy pickins?" Christ, she's adorable. "Can't have that."

"I've got my pride, Rux."

Maybe, but her confidence could sure use a bump.

"Okay, so our situation is this. You don't really want my kiss—which is crazy because it's amazing—

33

but you need it so The Blip knows you aren't desperate. Yeah?"

"Easy, stud. Your kiss was nice. But my bar is set pretty high."

My eyes narrow. "By who?"

If she tells me some high school boy from seven years ago who didn't know enough to hold on to what he had, I might have to make a point I was kind of hoping not to make.

"I don't kiss and tell," she says, eyes dancing with mischief.

Whatever.

"But, yes. So far as The Blip is concerned, you're my boyfriend now." She lets out a little squeak, grabbing my hand back for another crush. "He's turning around. Do it. Do it. Do it."

"Cammy—"

Poking me in the ribs, she steps closer. "Just suck it up and kiss me already." I haven't even moved in an inch when her hand pushes into my chest, holding me back. Her eyes are deathly serious. "And Rux, make it good."

As a rule, I'm all about giving this girl whatever she wants. She's had a tough run and making her smile is one of the better fucking things in life. But *making it good* probably isn't a great idea. That said, I've got another play in mind that might be.

"Cammy, chill." When she takes a breath, I catch her chin in the crook of my finger, bringing her eyes up to mine.

She stills.

I brush my thumb across the swell of her bottom lip. This girl has the hottest, tartest, sweetest mouth and it's kind of fun to get to play with it like this for a minute when I normally make a point of pushing those objective observations aside. Thinking about that sexy, soft lip too much could get a guy in trouble.

Cammy

RUX IS A BIG GUY. He's got muscles everywhere. Big hands. Big shoulders. An even bigger ego. But when the big goof puts his hands on me, he's incredibly gentle, brushing the hair from my eyes and tucking it behind my ear with such tender care, I melt a little.

It's not what I'm expecting from my showy friend.

"What are you doing?" I ask quietly, all too aware of how his hand hasn't moved away, and his thumb is stroking my cheek.

"Being a good boyfriend." He repeats the actions on the other side.

No one touches my hair, and the feel of his fingers

in it nearly has me moaning at the gentle tug. Trying to keep my focus, I whisper, "This kiss needs to say long-term tenderness and emotion. Then you'll never have to do it again."

He nods, the corner of his mouth twitching like he's finding this all so cute. He finds everything cute. Which is kind of cute itself, now that I think about it.

He's holding my face in the cradle of his palms. Like I'm precious. Like he never wants to let me go.

Like he's putting way more into this bit of fiction than I would have expected him to. Heck, the way he's touching me is almost enough to convince *me*.

I'm about to tell him to get on with it, but then he starts to move and I tip my head to his, my lips parting as I ready to take this kiss I really don't want… that I'm not waiting for… that's only about my dinged ego and a misplaced need to prove something to a guy I couldn't care less about.

His face is so close to mine, moving along the contours in this slow tease, his cheeks almost touching mine, noses nearly aligned, so close I can feel the heat from his skin, the wash of his breath against my lips, my jaw—oh my God—that tender skin beneath.

I swallow. Try to keep my breathing even, but this thing he's doing, this not-quite kiss that has my heart starting to skip and my belly starting to twist, is some seriously powerful stuff.

And he hasn't even kissed me yet. My lips are starting to tingle with the want of it. The needy pull getting stronger and stronger with every second he draws out his tease. His mouth is next to my ear, so close I get chills along my neck from the sensation of that charged bit of air occupying the space between us.

"Fuck this guy, Cammy," he murmurs softly. "He doesn't deserve a single thought."

I nod and the motion is enough to make contact, bringing his lips against the shell of my ear for one fleeting second. Just long enough for that low-level current to sizzle across my skin, drawing a quiet gasp from me.

Chuckling softly, Rux pulls back.

One brow raised in a look so cocky and sure, at any other time I'd have to give him trouble for it. But today, after this?

"Wow. You have got some serious game."

He nods. "I know, right?"

"I mean, my belly feels like I just stepped off the Eagle up at Six Flags and do you see this?" Tipping my head to the side, I show him my neck.

"Chills? You're a sensitive little thing."

I guess. "Hey, you didn't kiss me."

He gives me another grin so smug I can't help but smile along with him. "Pretty sure I got the message across anyway."

He's right. Relieved, I beam up at him. "You're *so* into me. It's totally obvious."

"Yep." And then he rests his hand over mine… where I've fisted his shirt against his heart. "And it's not one-sided."

Seeing what I've done, my brows shoot high as I blush, smoothing the fabric with a few pats of my hand. "Guess not."

"You good to get out of here?" he asks, buttoning my jacket.

I nod and we head out, probably passing The Blip at the door. But honestly, I've sort of lost track of him.

Outside, Rux throws a heavy arm around my shoulders and pulls me in, keeping me warm.

"Thanks for that, Rux."

"You bet."

When we get to his truck, I climb in and buckle up while he starts the engine. He turns to me. "What?"

"Gotta admit, now I'm wondering what kind of kiss you're packing when you actually try."

Shaking his head with a laugh, he pulls into traffic. "I bet you are. And guess what?"

I raise a brow.

"You owe me. We're watching *Oak Island*."

Chapter 4

Cammy

I can barely look at myself in the mirror. Last night was… it was nothing. Except somehow my sex-starved subconscious disagrees and is making a bigger deal out of that not-quite kiss that was strictly for show than it should.

I've never had a dirty dream about Rux before. Ever. Not even before we were really friends and all I knew about him was that he was this big, sexy hockey star who hung out with my sister's secret boyfriend. Granted, there'd been a lot on my mind back then. And by the time I'd sorted it out, Rux had become a regular in my life. He'd become my friend. One I needed more than any kind of sexual fantasy.

So no naughty dreams about Rux.

Until last night. When suddenly he shows up in my dreams cast in a role he's never played before. What's worse? It's not like I even got any action out of it. It was just this replay of the events from the night before, only instead of being sort of delightfully giddy and quietly awed by Rux's ladies' man skill set... I was completely caught up in the closeness of our bodies, the way his mouth hovered so near mine, the electric charge sizzling between us.

I wanted more.

But even as my breath went uneven and my pulse sped, he continued to torment me, tease me—moving into that space just beyond my reach. Tempting me with what I couldn't have.

Making me beg his name and whisper pleas he wouldn't answer.

All he'd give me was that knowing eye contact, that heavy-lidded stare.

Until I'd woken reaching into the empty space of my bedroom, breathless and worked up to a near painful degree. I'm ashamed to admit I thought about Bob. But there was no way I could give in to that impulse with Rux on the brain—Rux!

Uncool.

So very, very, very uncool.

And now Rux is on his way over and not only am I wondering how I'll be able to look at myself in the mirror… but how am I going to be able to look him in the eye?

The sound of the door opening says it's too late to figure it out.

I head into the living room telling myself it's going to be fine.

Seriously, this is Rux.

The guy has zero filter and doesn't seem to understand the concept of TMI.

There is no reason to be concerned. None.

The only reason it will get weird is if I make it that way.

"Morning, Sunshine. How'd you sleep?"

I could totally dodge the question. Answer fine and move on. But the idea of keeping a stupid dream a secret feels like I'd be giving it more power, making it more of a thing than if I just put it out there.

We'll have a laugh. He'll tease me while his ego bloats to monumental proportions. I'll find a way to put a pin in it. We'll get on with our day.

"That good, huh?" He drops onto the couch, setting down the coffees and pastry bag on the coffee table first. "Got you a banana nirvana thing this morning," he says, looking completely delighted as he waves his hand over the sip hole, wafting the scent toward his nose.

"That sounds gross, but I'm kind of curious

anyway." I drop onto the couch beside him, tucking one knee on the cushions between us as I take the steaming insulated mug. "Oh wow, that really does smell good."

He's nodding, his smile getting bigger by the minute.

This guy is so much fun. He devours new experiences like no one I've ever met before, and I have to admit, it's not bad getting caught in the wake of that excitement.

I take a sip and my brows pop up as my mouth goes into meltdown mode over how delicious it is. "Wow. I totally thought that was going to be a bust, but it might be my new favorite drink."

I hand him the cup. He takes a sip and falls back against the couch cushions with a groan that ought to be contained to the bedroom and has me wanting to kick myself for letting my head go there.

Rux is my friend. I don't want to be thinking about the sounds he makes in the bedroom. Not at all. But here I am, staring at the sprawl of his long legs, the way his heavy thighs fill out his red athletic pants and his vintage Easton T-shirt stretches over the ridged terrain of his abs.

"What's wrong? Funky aftertaste?" He smacks his lips, brows furrowing in concentration. "Still tastes good to me."

"No, the coffee is delicious. It was just…" I think about the way he'd been looking at me in my dream the night before and feel my cheeks flame.

Catching my wrist, he sits up, grin slanting like it's a hairsbreadth from slipping off his face. "Just what?"

Meeting his eyes, I shake my head and let out a strained breath. Which I hate, because there's nothing strained between us. It's always easy and open and— and I'm not going to be the one to screw that up by turning *nothing* into something bigger than it should be.

"This is silly and you're never going to let me live it down, but…"

One thick brow pushes up.

I take a breath and bite the bullet.

"But you got all up in my head with your not-quite kiss last night, and I had a dirty dream about you." The words spill out in a rush and I'm pretty sure I'm going to die of embarrassment. Except then Rux barks out a laugh, eyes glittering with smug satisfaction.

"Oh my God, you don't have to laugh about it," I gasp, but I'm already joining him as relief floods me.

How does he do it? Know exactly what I need even before I do.

"I'm not!" he shouts out, setting the coffee aside as I poke at his ribs a few times. He catches my hand and pulls me into him so I fall against his chest.

It's a place I've been a hundred times before, and

I'm not going to think about it any differently now. Even if it is a pretty spectacular place to land.

"Okay, maybe I was a little."

I pinch his ribs and using some superhuman hockey-stud strength, he tucks me along his side, so I'm beneath his arm and half between him and the back of the couch, half on top of him.

Again, it's a place I've been a hundred times before. It's one of my favorite ways to be when we're watching a movie after Matty's gone to bed or we're just talking and Rux wants a cuddle.

Now, his big arm is holding me tight, keeping me close as he lets out a contented sigh.

"So how was I?" he asks, tucking his chin to give me a salacious grin. "I was a stallion, right? Rocked your world right off its axis."

I huff out a laugh, beyond grateful that I told him and that he found exactly the right way to diffuse any tension I might have been holding onto about it.

"You were a freaking tease."

He stills and then pulls back again. "Huh?"

"Yeah, it was all that same business you were giving me last night, except times ten. And then you were giving me these sexy eyes that, I'm not going to lie, were pretty potent."

He pulls back even farther, a deep furrow etched

between his brows. "The same business like we didn't even kiss?"

"You wouldn't give it up. I wanted it, bad. But no. You weren't accommodating."

That big arm clamps around me again and he smiles into my hair. "Total bullshit on my part, Sunshine. Sorry."

I burrow into his side a little deeper, and sigh. "It was BS, but I forgive you."

"Dream Rux sounds like a dick. Pretty uncool considering..."

I'm so relaxed, I think I could fall asleep right where I am. But there's something about the way he's left that sentence...

Lifting my head, I meet his eyes. "Considering what?"

Oh yeah, that smile is every kind of unrepentant naughty. "Dream Cammy *always* puts out."

Cammy

"HE DID NOT SAY THAT!" Julia practically shouts through the line as I poke around my desk, pushing my little stack of heart-shaped sticky notes in line with the high-heel tape dispenser.

"He totally did. And worse yet, then he winked! And now, he's been sending me these lip-pics all afternoon."

"What the hell is a lip-pic?"

"Like a dick-pic but featuring his dirty mouth instead of his package." I roll my eyes just thinking about the assortment of pictures of Rux's lips filling up my phone. "Here, sending you one now… At first I thought he'd accidentally fumbled the phone, somehow snapped the picture, and sent, but then I got the next one." And the next after that.

I wait for it, and yeah, my sister's squeal says she got it.

"Hello, he's biting his lip."

"But just a little." Not like he's trying to chew the thing off.

"Yeah, sort of tasteful but still sexy."

"That's what I told him!" I love those moments when Julia and I share the same brain. She's six years older than I am, and we don't even have the same dad —but we're close in a way that comes from her stepping in and raising me whenever our mom wasn't up for the task. So most of the time.

"There's another one in here with just a hint of tongue. Like barely any… but it's so dirty!"

Julia and I dissect a few more of the pictures before I hear Greg getting curious from her end of the line.

Less than a minute later, I've got a text from Rux, because those two are like twelve-year-old girls.

Rux: Those were private pictures. I can't believe you shared them.

And of course it's punctuated with a little lip emoji that looks like an exclamation mark.

Cammy: My phone was hacked.

Rux: The internet is forever.

"Hey, pay attention to me," Julia teases through the line. "You can text with Rux anytime."

"Sorry, sorry!" I say, snapping a quick picture of my own lips, wide and smiling, and even though I'm not wearing any lipstick, shoot it off to Rux. "So when are you guys leaving for LA anyway?"

With Greg out for the foreseeable future, he's going with Julia while she shoots her show.

"Tomorrow night. I'll be out there for two weeks but Greg might come back early. Hey, how'd it go with Matty at Jeremy's last night?"

And like that, my good humor dies. Stepping out of my office, I glance down the hall to my son's door. "Good. He brought the cooler back empty, so his dad could keep the snacks for next time he came over. And when he got home, he talked about a mile a minute about playing cards and board games."

Julia's more reserved now as well. "That's nice he had fun."

"It is," I agree, knowing that neither one of us really loves it all that much. Even if we both want Matty to be able to have the kind of relationship with his father that neither of us had with ours, it's still a little hard to get that excited about my son bonding with a man that, deep down, I'm worried will leave him again.

"When's Matty going next?"

"He's going to sleep over the weekend after next, but I think Jeremy will see him for a few hours next Saturday with his parents."

"How's it going with the GPs now that he's back?"

"It's a little weird actually. Like maybe they aren't sure how close they should be with me. I don't know. Maybe that isn't fair, but it feels like every time I've seen them since he said he was coming home his mom has been looking at me differently."

"You think she's worried you won't let Jeremy back into Matty's life the way she wants you to?"

Possibly. Jeremy's parents have never been my biggest fans. When we dated in high school they were kind and welcoming, but there was a coolness, a detachment there. And when I got pregnant, it changed to something more like blame.

At the time, it was disappointing because I'd always dreamed of being a part of a big, warm, loving family and it was clear that wasn't the case with the

Levensons. And when Jeremy left me—well, I didn't see them again for a year. Not until they reached out, wanting to have a relationship with their grandson.

"I think she's just trying to figure out how this is going to affect her relationship with Matty. They've been taking him every other Friday night for the last four years. Now Jeremy is and"—I sigh, shaking my head—"there's only so much time I'm willing to give my son up. So yes, it's going to be different."

"You can't feel bad about that, Cam."

My heart pangs and I nod. "I know. It's just a little hard sometimes when life feels like it's slipping out of my control. I want something better for Matty than we had. And before Jeremy decided to move back I kind of thought I might be giving it to him. He didn't have a dad, but he had everything else. He had stability. He felt safe. And now that Jeremy's back, he's getting the dad part but that security feels like it's slipping through my fingers."

"Hey, I know what that feels like and I know how scary it is. But this isn't going to be another repeat of what happened throughout our childhood. This is going to be fine. You and Matty have a support structure here that Mom never could have dreamed of and wouldn't have even wanted. It's going to be fine."

"I love you, Julia."

"Love you too, kiddo."

Chapter 5

Rux

*W*e're almost out of time. Down by two with less than five minutes on the clock, and I'm off. Out of sync with the guys, missing shots I shouldn't be missing. I'm a half-second behind, when I need to be ahead, and it's costing us the game, damn it.

Twisting back, I untangle my stick from Halson's, pushing off hard to get free, to get open. There's a blink when I'm looking to where Greg should be, only I'm lined up with Vassar and O'Brian and instead of just knowing where they are on an instinctual level, I've got to find them. Get to where they can find me.

It happens, but I can't miss that half-second delay

that feels wrong in every fucking way. Even when I knock the puck out of the air and carry it up the ice, even when I find that sliver of space between the guys dogging my heels and the teammate powering into position. Even when the puck lands on his stick and a single flick of his wrist later, the net lights up and the crowd goes wild—I can't shake that half-second delay because it feels like the reason we're still down a point instead of rocking a lead.

It's the reason we don't win.

Everyone's got too much aggression bottled up inside. We're pissed because this is a game we should have won. Could have won, if things were gelling between the players more consistently... If I could bring it together.

I hate this feeling of letting the guys down. I know they wouldn't say I did and I know they'd tell me it takes more than one player to make a team. But I also know what it feels like when that connection is locked down. When that half second is on your side instead of working against you.

By the time I get past the interviews and heart-to-heart with Coach, I'm not in any mood to hang out. At least not with the guys I let down tonight. What I want is to head back to Cammy's place and sit on the couch and hear about her day. I want to know who

Matty hung out with at recess and whether the tortellini bake she was trying off Pinterest was actually as good as scratch lasagna. I want to chill and relax in a way I don't get to with anyone but her.

But Cammy was at the game tonight. And we have plans to meet at the Five Hole. So that's where I'm going.

I walk into the bar with Vassar and get a slightly more subdued version of our normal greeting. There are still cheers and back slaps, and guys and girls I've never laid eyes on before edging up into my space to tell me what a fan they are. And I know what a lucky schmuck I am, so even though tonight I'm really not in the mood to shake all the hands and smile at all the compliments I don't feel like I deserve, I do it anyway.

Finally, I clear the front end of the bar, and once I reach the back, the crowd peels off. It's sort of an unwritten rule in the Five Hole and the main reason most of the guys come here—once we're past that first open area, we're allowed to be guys out for a beer. People don't approach us for handshakes or selfies, they don't ask for autographs.

Cammy's at the back end of the bar with Natalie, and just seeing her there decked out in my number, head tilted back, eyes glittering as she laughs at something Nat said, is enough to loosen the vise of tension around my chest. Vassar places a hand on my shoulder and edges past to swoop in on his girl. Grabbing four beers off the bar, Cammy finds me with that smile I can't get enough of.

And it's all good.

I take one of the beers and sling an arm around her slim shoulders, pulling her in for a hug as we walk over to our usual table.

"Matty get over to Teddy's okay?" It's not Jeremy's week but Matty got invited to a sleepover at his best friend's house for the night.

"Yes, Sally texted to let me know they tore into the Legos the second they got there and didn't stop until they went to bed." She holds up her phone and I can't help but grin at the picture of the little dude with his buddy surrounded by a sea of tiny bricks.

"Check out the speeder, *nice*."

"He's been building them over and over since you showed him how. He's very proud of his new skill."

I sit taller and dust off my shoulders. "I'm badass with the Legos."

Cammy thumbs to the next picture, Matty conked out on the rollaway bed in Teddy's room, his face peaceful, hair a little messy over his brow.

"Damn, you made a cute kid."

She smiles beside me and I find out all the shit I

like to hear about from her day, like the funny-as-hell outtake Julia shared from taping with one of the rookie Bears players. The guy was so nervous he ended up spilling a cup of coffee down her chest and then was so mortified he tried wiping it up.

"And his face is like purple by this point and she keeps telling him it's okay and the producers are swarming the set, but he won't give them the napkins. And I mean this kid is practically cupping her boob"—she's holding her hands up, pantomiming the whole thing with this frantic look on her face—"and it's like you can see in his horrified eyes that he knows he's making it worse but he just can't stop."

This is what I needed.

Only then Cammy's face loses some of its light. I follow her eyes to where the bar opens up, and a few people down from Vassar and Nat is The Blip.

"Jesus, this guy is everywhere."

The muscles that had barely begun to unlock are suddenly winding tight again. That feeling of futility and exasperation pushing into my chest.

Except unlike with the game, I'm pretty sure I can do something about this.

Cammy sits back in her chair and takes a swallow of her beer. "Forget about him. I have."

"I will." I reach out and brush a wayward curl

from her face, tucking that bit of blonde behind her ear. "Right after this."

"Right after what?" Her eyes go a little wider, like on some level she already knows.

Letting the backs of my knuckles stroke against the silky skin of her cheek, I lean closer. "Right after I make my point." And I lean in the rest of the way and kiss her.

Cammy

RUX'S KISS is a soft press so different from that first showy thing a few weeks ago, I barely recognize the connection. While that kiss had been sudden, a press of body parts in an almost clinical way—this feels infinitely different.

Maybe it's the way he looked at me, searching my eyes before moving in. Or the tender touch that set my nerve endings on edge. Or maybe it's just that I could read in his eyes what he was going to do and after last week with that not-quite kiss I was the tiniest bit more curious than I should have been.

But instead of delivering a cold shock of surprise, this kiss warms me, sending tendrils of heat through my lips and across my skin. Sparking an awareness I'm not supposed to feel with my best friend, but that's so good and nice and different from anything I've felt in years… I lean into it instead of pulling away.

One big hand sifts into the hair at the back of my neck and the other gently cups my jaw, holding me as he tastes my lips again. The contact lingers before breaking as his hand glides down the length of my neck to just below my collar bone, trailing more of that nerve-stirring warmth in its wake.

It feels good. Maybe a little too good.

My eyes lift slowly, because *wow.*

Catching my hand in his, he threads our fingers together, holding them against his thigh like we're—

"Total boyfriend move," he murmurs, cocking his head toward mine. "Right?"

A soft sigh slips past my still-tingling lips and I touch the fingers of my free hand to them. "Definitely a boyfriend move."

So much so that I can feel the wires starting to cross in my mind. The line that's always been so clear I never had to even think about it before… smudging just a little.

And I see it.

Rux would be a really nice boyfriend for someone.

For the right girl. At the right time. If he ever decided that was what he wanted.

"Thought about going all in, doing the devouring-your-mouth-like-a-starving-man business." He's rubbing the back of my hand with his thumb while he talks—light strokes, soft circles. "But that's more like heat-of-the-moment stuff. So I went understated instead."

I nod, trying not to think about those little circles. The tingles spreading from that contained touch. The heat unfurling in my belly as Rux casually discusses his choice of kiss. I try not to think about what that other version might have been like.

"Seems like the right call. I'm impressed." And while I don't feel quite as casual about it as I make it sound, I really am.

He looks down at where our hands are locked together over his mountain of a thigh and then grins at me again. "This is nice. The hand-holding. Would it be weird if I wanted to do it all the time?"

I give him a squeeze. "Not at all."

Vaughn and Nat slide into the seats across from us, and Vaughn raises a brow. "You two holding hands under the table?"

Rux nods. "We're a couple. Totally into each other on a more than physical level."

Natalie sits back in her chair with a delighted smile and asks, "Wow, so this is getting serious then, huh?"

"Hell, yeah, it is. Three-week anniversary tonight. Figured I'd bring her back to where it all started."

I almost spit out my beer and, looking to the guy who makes me laugh like no one else, cock my head. "He's so sentimental."

"She's got it bad for me. Thinking about those three little words." He leans in toward our friends. "I'm ready to introduce her to my mom. It's not too soon, is it, Sunshine?"

"I've met your mom. Twice." She's like a mellowed version of her son… but still totally over the top.

Rux rubs my hand against his thigh, angling his body toward me again. "Yeah, she loves you. Maybe we can Skype her one of these nights when Matty's home."

From across the table, Vaughn is shaking his head. "You guys are nuts."

Maybe a little. My eyes cut to Rux. Maybe a lot. But I wouldn't have it any other way.

Rux finally lets my hand go. We haven't seen The Blip since before the quality-boyfriend-kiss incident, but Rux isn't giving up the pretense. He drops a kiss on my hand before going up to grab another beer for Nat and me, and the minute he sits back down he pulls me into his side like he always does—except not quite like always. My back rests against his side, and where his arm would normally be hooked behind me, this time, it loops over my shoulder, so our hands are tucked together in the vicinity of my heart.

Nat and Vaughn give us shit about it, but the whole thing feels so natural, it's all too easy to forget it isn't real. That Rux doesn't always hold my hand or play with my hair. That prior to this night, there existed an inch of space between us.

Chapter 6

Rux

"Y ou ready to get out of here?" I ask as Cammy yawns into her hand. She's still tucked into my side, closer than I normally get to cuddle her, and not gonna lie. It's pretty nice.

"Oh, yeah, sure. If you are." She sits straight, eyes sharp as she scans the crowd around us.

Ahh. Looking for The Blip. Probably wondering what kind of no-brain move I'm going to make on the way out of here. Not that I can really blame her after the liberties I've taken tonight. I'm lucky she didn't take my head off for stealing another kiss.

But it's kind of stuck in my craw that she was worried that one kiss would make her look like fair game for a one-nighter. Even with as little time as I spent with that guy, most people pick up on the fact that I'm pretty protective of Cammy real quick. And even if she was feeling vulnerable, no way would I let anyone—not a teammate, not a buddy, and not myself—anywhere close enough to take advantage.

And I'm not going to let some asshole too dumb to see what kind of once-in-a-lifetime opportunity he had within his grasp think it either.

Still, fun driving the point home. But it's not something Cammy needs to worry about a repeat performance of after tonight.

"Pretty sure he left already," I say, running a hand over her shoulder. "Saw him and those two dipshits he always hangs around with headed for the door when I grabbed the beers earlier."

I'm half expecting her to lay into me for keeping the pretense up when we didn't need to. But I've already got my defense lined up, so she can bring it. What if he had *other* friends at the bar? What would they think if it was hands-off the second that guy walked out the door?

It's a legit excuse, but not the primary one.

Snuggling in with Cammy just feels good. And while I get physical affection from her on the regular, this is different. I like holding her hand. Touching her hair. Hell, I like kissing that soft, sweet mouth of hers. But none of that is really cool for friends to do, unless they've got a damn good excuse.

As it happens... I do.

Yeah, I'm still going to be just as relentless about shutting down any stray thoughts that cross the line as I always am. But I'm also going to enjoy this for as long as I've got it. Because it's *nice*.

"They left?" she asks.

"Pretty sure."

Her spine softens and with the way her shoulders droop and her eyes skate away—that can't be right—she almost looks… *disappointed?*

"You okay?"

As quickly as whatever that look was appeared, it's gone. And then she's smiling at me. Grabbing her coat and letting me help her into it.

Nat and Vassar have already left, so we say goodbye to Diesel and Grady who are huddled up at the end of the bar.

Once we're in the truck, she turns to me. "You make a pretty good boyfriend, Rux."

"So long as no one actually has to count on me for anything."

She shakes her head and, even though I know it's true, I like that she disagrees.

Pulling into traffic, I start toward her place.

"Thought I was going to have to take another jabby finger-beating for sneaking that kiss."

I catch the roll of her eyes and then change lanes.

"What? No. That kiss was nice. Like you said, perfect boyfriend kiss."

"I've got skills, babe."

We're stopped for a light when I glance over, ready for whatever cut-down she's about to deliver to my ego. But there's something in the way she turns away that puts my spidey senses on alert.

"What's with that look?" Shit, maybe she really did think my kiss was bad. That first time I wasn't fucking trying. But that kiss tonight was nice. Better than nice. Hell, it was harder than I'd expected to stop because it was so nice. "You still think I suck at kissing."

"What?" she croaks, then covers her face with her hands. "Umm… no. You definitely don't suck."

"So what's with all… this?" I wave my hand in front of her face.

A deep breath and then she's adjusting in her seat so she's facing me more. "God, like your ego really needs any more inflating."

Now she's got my attention. "It really does. Just one more pump, please."

I'm being an ass, but she loves me anyway. And I want to know what's up. After a little huff of breath, she looks out the windshield and sighs. "Your kiss is actually so very good, I was maybe a little… disappointed The Blip left after the first one."

This time it's my brow pushing up. I sit a little straighter. "Why's that?"

Yeah, I know. But I want to hear her say it.

Instead I get a swat on the arm and her muttering under her breath.

Damn, she's cute.

"Sorry, missed that. What were you saying?"

Swat, swat.

"So you were hoping for another taste of the good stuff before we left the bar. One not-quite-real kiss and you're hooked, huh?"

Her arms cross over her chest, but she's not fooling me. Not when she can't fight that smile to save her life.

"Please. I wanted one more kiss. *One.* I haven't had a decent kiss in forever. And I just thought… if I had a good excuse… maybe it wouldn't be so bad to try out one of your other signature kisses. That's all."

That's enough to keep the smile on my face for the rest of the ride back to her place.

I luck out with a spot on her block and walk her into her building. The guy at the desk, Saul, I think, waves and tells us to have a good night. I'll be back down after Cammy's inside her apartment, and chances are he'll bring up the game before I go.

In the elevator, I look down at Cammy's hand by

her side and kind of wish I could hold it again. Just because it's nice. Nothing else.

When we get to her door, I use my own key but then stop Cammy before she goes inside.

"Not coming in?" she asks.

And damn, I want to. But something tells me it's a better idea to go home.

"Not tonight." But instead of backing down the hall with the promise to call her tomorrow, I lean into the frame of the door and give myself permission to look at her like the woman she is instead of the friend who means more to me than the world.

There's a blink of confusion in her eyes as they meet mine, but it's gone with the catch of her breath.

This woman is my best friend, but I'd be lying if I said that sound didn't get to me.

Snaring my favorite wayward curl, I tuck that blonde rebel behind her ear and let my fingers linger there.

"What are you doing?" she whispers.

Sliding my hand around the back of her silky neck, I let my mouth fall into the hooked smile that's always gotten results with the girls.

"What do you think I'm doing?"

Cammy

"OH MY GOD. You're going to kiss me." My heart starts to skip, my eyes racing over him from that sexy-as-sin smile I've seen him use with other girls, but never on me, to the sort of casual stance that somehow makes his already impossibly broad shoulders even broader, and the eyes that look like they've got a secret behind them… one that I'll be very lucky to learn.

He's totally going to kiss me.

His other hand comes up to cup my jaw, thumb brushing feather light over my cheek as his fingers thread into my hair. The sensation of being held like this is overwhelming. Intoxicating. So very good, I'm afraid to breathe for fear it will signal the end and this gentle, intimate touch will go away.

But then he's tipping my head back. And the eyes that were locked with mine lower to my mouth. "What's one more, right?" he says quietly, deep voice rumbling low as he closes the distance between us. "A last little bit of kissing fun between friends, yeah?"

"Yeah," I breathe, and I want him to kiss me. Maybe all passionate and devouring like he'd mentioned. But just thinking about it has this giddy squeal working up my throat and my hand pops up between us. "Wait, give me a second. I don't want to be giggling when you do it. If this is the last one, I want it to be good."

Rux keeps his gentle hold on me, his gruff laugh sounding as I try to push the smile off my face, but when it won't quite die, I sigh. "You're the best, Rux."

"The best kisser?" Oh, he's so smug. He'll be insufferable after this.

"No. Just the best." I tug at his shirt and do a little shake. "Okay, I'm ready. Gimme, gimme, gimme."

There's pure affection in his smile, and once again I'm reminded why I'm so lucky to count this man as my friend.

"Okay, Sunshine. Last one."

I nod. His eyes crinkle at the corners as a warm breath spills over my lips a second before contact. It starts with a tease. A taste. A breath. The barest rub of his lips against mine. A shiver breaks over my skin at the feel of his fingers in my hair, the light tension against my scalp, and I can feel him smile in response.

And then he kisses me, *really* kisses me, and whatever lingering giggle was there a second ago is wiped away beneath the sensations flaring to life at every point of contact between us. Rux is a really good kisser. Confident, skilled, and sure.

I never thought he'd be bad. But I had no idea it would be like *this*.

I wasn't prepared. And it's... overwhelming.

Addicting. Because God, I want *more*. I want him to keep kissing me like this until our mouths don't work anymore and all we can do is collapse into a heap on the couch together.

I want to make the most of this stolen moment, that's both outside our friendship and in.

I try to stay passive, not take more than he's giving, but it's been so long since I had a kiss anywhere close to this. And then my hands are against his chest, smoothing up his dress shirt and slipping around his neck. Which must be okay, because he lets out this rough groan and snakes his arm around me, pulling me into the hard-packed muscles of his body, tight and then tighter. My hands are in his hair, and it's thick and feels incredible tangled around my fingers and clutched within my fist… spilling around my face when he bows me back.

He takes my mouth completely. Our tongues roll in a slow, wet glide that has my heart slamming and that place deep in my center aching with a need that makes me feel so alive, so good it startles the smallest whimper out of me.

This is the hottest kiss of my life.

His mouth moves to that sensitive, long-neglected spot beneath my jaw and he *sucks*.

Heat spills through my center in a rush as I gasp, "*Rux*."

"Do you want me to stop?" he asks, brushing his lips over that same wicked spot.

"No, no, no, no, nooo, don't stop," I plead in a squeaky rush that earns me another gruff rumble, this one buried in the crook of my neck. And that, the sound of his laughter in the midst of this heat… that's a dangerous sound, one a girl could get used to.

I won't. I know better. Rux has made it clear where his lines are drawn. That the life I dream about isn't for him. Or at least, not as the leading man.

But for the next minute or so, I'm going to enjoy all he has to give me.

"You want more, greedy girl?" he teases, his tongue snaking a path up the column of my neck.

"Yes," I pant as chills break out across the skin I'm shamelessly offering him. Though what *more* looks like, I can't even imagine because this feels like *everything*. This feels like the hottest, dirtiest, most body-and-soul, all-encompassing kiss of my life.

Rux guides me back against the wall beside my door and pins my wrists over my head with one hand before running the other down my arm, my ribs, waist, and hip. My heart is racing, my body on fire. Some distant tiny voice in my head warns that we should stop, but then he's kissing me again, giving me his tongue in a series of slow, sexy thrusts that have me thinking thoughts I'm not supposed to have about this man.

Dirty thoughts.

Sweaty thoughts.

Deep, pounding, delicious thoughts.

Moaning around the thrust of his tongue, I slip my hands free of his hold. They're on his arms, in in his hair, testing the resistance of his insanely hard pecs. I can't get enough of this man's body beneath my touch, the taste of him. Our kiss flames hotter and hotter until whatever semblance of control there'd been between us is completely burned away and—

Rux rears back, brows pulled together over dark eyes blazing with a heat that's never been between us before.

My hands are shaking and I can't catch my breath. This is crazy. I should let go, pull my hands out of his hair and peel my body back from his. At the very least, stop staring into his eyes like I never want to look away.

But I've been so good, so very responsible all these years. And this—

"*Cammy.*" This is not my friend looking back at me, and for once I don't want him to be.

My breath catches on a little whimper and then he does it—grabs me by the back of my neck and pulls me in hard.

Chapter 7

Cammy

$\mathcal{W}$e come together in a bruising crush, hands and mouths everywhere, feet tangling together as we stumble into the apartment. My back meets the wall inside the door and less than a second later he's there, his big hand roaming over my ass in a possessive rub that ends with another deeply appreciative growl against my throat.

That sound. It makes me wild, makes me ache. Makes me frantic to get us where we're going before either of us has a chance to think enough to stop. Because friends don't do this, do they?

It feels like there are reasons. Evidence, maybe. But then Rux has my knee hitched at his side and he's filling the space he's made with his body.

Friends can *totally* do this.

At least friends as good as we are.

He tips my hips to meet him, the contact just so and— "Rux!"

My fingers dig into his shoulders and we're mindless, breathless, rocking into each other like teenagers. Except even back in high school, when it felt like I would die if I didn't get closer to Jeremy, it was nothing like this.

It's *never* been like this.

"You're ruining me," I gasp, tugging the shirt I've already got half the buttons undone on free of his suit pants. I can't stand the clothes between us, need to feel his skin. "Don't stop."

Shoot, that might have been a button popping, but Rux doesn't seem to mind and, finally, his shirt is hanging open over that insanely cut chest. Wow. I'm totally going to run my tongue between the grooves of his abs.

My jersey goes next, but his number hasn't even hit the floor before Rux pulls back and stills. His eyes rake over me and he wipes a hand over his mouth.

"Jesus, you're killing me." Hands skimming up my waist and ribs, he pauses at the wire of my bra, takes a breath, and then cups my oversensitive breasts in his palms and groans out a string of unintelligible praise that has my belly folding in on itself with need.

"I keep telling myself to stop, Sunshine. Not to take this too far. That I shouldn't want you like this… but one taste and I'm dying for you." His thumbs brush over the tight peaks of my straining nipples once, twice… He meets my eyes. "Tell me I'm not making a mistake with you. Tell me I'm not risking *us* here, because if I am— Tell me to walk the hell away. I'll show up with coffee and donuts tomorrow and we'll yak it up over what a douche I was tonight."

My heart breaks a little with how much this man means to me. "No risk, and you're not a douche. You're perfect." I cover his hands with mine, encouraging him to keep going. To touch me more. Make me feel the things I tell myself I can live without.

"We're friends and that isn't going to change because you're giving me something I don't get a lot of in my life."

Rux searches my eyes, and whatever he finds in them has the corner of his mouth pulling up into another panty-melting smile. "So, I should probably make you come then."

Oh God, the confidence in that statement is so hot. "You should totally do that."

Continuing to play with my nipple with one hand, the other dips into my leggings. My breath fractures at the flick of his wrist and slow tease of his fingers, first over my panties and then under.

He's doing that *not quite* thing again, hovering close, but not quite giving me what I want... making me want it even more. His mouth is so close to my ear, I can feel the heat of his breath, those tiny static charges arcing between his lips and my skin... His fingers so close to my pussy, I'm starting to shake.

"Are you wet for me, Sunshine?" The low rumble of his voice works through me, settling low in my belly like a warm weight.

I nod, my eyes locked on the hard cut of his jaw, the smattering of stubble, and the sexy twist of his lips. I'm soaked. Aching.

"Good girl."

I shouldn't like it, but I'm closer to coming from those two words alone than the last guy I slept with ever got me.

And then one blunt finger brushes over me—"So soft."—and my knees almost give out.

I clutch his arm, his shoulder. Whimper as that single thick digit follows the slick seam of my sex, parting me and then slowly pushing inside. "*Rux.*"

"So wet... So hot." Pumping in and out, he adds a second finger and, bringing his mouth back to mine, licks inside. "So *tight*. Christ, I can already feel you gripping me." Another deep stroke... another shuddering gasp as the tension builds. "You going to come all over my fingers?"

Biting my lip hard enough to draw blood, I nod.

I'm close. So close. My breath broken and ragged, my body straining toward every touch, every dirty word. Toward Rux and what he's doing to me and how badly I want it.

"You want me to fuck you?" He thrusts again, curving his fingers just so to reach that impossible place deep inside. *Rubbing.*

"*Rux,*" I plead, the need twisting hard, knotting in on itself until I can barely breathe. Until I'm rocking over his hand, panting into his mouth, teetering at the brink of—

His thumb comes down on my clit in a firm press, and I cry out his name as I tip over the edge to the low rumble of Rux's dirty praise in my ear.

My body is still being slammed by waves of pleasure when he murmurs, "Better than Bob?"

I give up a breathless laugh. Everyone knows about Bob. But only Rux would bring him up now.

His tongue flicks against the lobe of my ear as the last waves of orgasm retreat. "You better tell me yes, or I'm going to make him watch what I do to you next."

Slumped against the wall, I loosen my fingers from his arm and sigh. "So much better than Bob."

And I'm definitely ruined, but before I can think about it too much, Rux presses a searing kiss to my lips, then ducks down and tosses me over his shoulder.

"Rux!" I squeal as he totes me through the apartment he knows as well as his own.

"Come on, babe. Let's go break your headboard."

Rux

THAT MOAN. Christ. Watching Cammy go off like that? I'm not going to forget that look on her face for as long as I live. I need to see it again.

I don't normally let myself acknowledge it, but Cammy has the finest ass. And I'm helping myself to it by the handful as I carry her, laughing and squirming, over my shoulder back to her room.

I bounce her onto the bed and she scoots back, resting on her elbows. Blonde curls spill around her face, and her lips part in this sort of breathless, sexy smile I'm going to beat it to for years. Prowling up after her, I land a kiss on that gorgeous mouth and give her a taste of my tongue.

And when she's arching beneath me and I'm hard enough to hammer nails, I back off the bed and start peeling her leggings down her luscious hips. I'm more distracted by the hot-as-fuck look on her face than anything else, but then I catch a glimpse of blue and gold and—

Holy hell. *Her panties.*

"Cammy, you don't even want to know how many decades of dirty fantasies are coming true right now."

"What?" She blinks in confusion. Then her head pops up, eyes wide. "Wait," she squeaks, hands covering all those stars and the double-W emblem. "I didn't think anyone would see these. I didn't even think about what I was pulling out of the drawer."

"Babe, I love Wonder Woman." I strip off her leggings the rest of the way, dying for another glimpse, but all I can see around her hands is the sort of scanty boy-shorts cut. I like them a lot. "I've beat it to her way more than you want to know. So the superhero panties aren't just adorable—they also got me so hard it hurts. Lemme see."

"It's not just the superhero thing." Her cheeks flame.

"No?" My mind goes to a million awesomely dirty scenarios. And now I really want to see them.

Knee between her legs, I try to nudge her hands away. And when that doesn't work, I start licking a path up her thigh. "Please? I'll show you mine if you show me yours."

"Julia bought them as a joke, okay?"

"Mm-hmm," I assure, swirling my tongue over the skin on her thigh until her hands retreat from that place I'm about to devour and— *What does that say?*

No way.

Raising a brow, I look up to Cammy, who's beet-red, covering as much of her face as she can.

Wonder Woman seeking Man Of Steel. Apply within.

Rubbing at the smile that's not going anywhere, I shake my head. "The arrow pointing down is a nice touch. Really clarifies things."

Groaning, she tries to roll over and hide even more, but I catch her hips and pull her back.

"Cammy, babe, you're not going to believe this."

She peeks through the vee of her fingers as I undo my fly and drop my pants.

Her hands move from her eyes to that sexy mouth as she gapes at my *man of steel*, straining against the Superman boxer briefs he's ready to bust through.

"*Shut the front door.*"

"I know, right?"

I want a picture so bad. But no way am I going to ask my single-mom best friend to let me take a picture of her three quarters of the way naked. I'd never share that shit, but—

"Get me the phone," she pleads, her brows going high. "Julia's going to die."

"You're going to call her? *Now?*" About this?

"No! But… we've got to take a picture. Not your face, of course."

"Wait, you're worried about my *face*?"

Her eyes track down and get a little hazy. "Okay, so maybe we should do something about that first." She bites her lip, and for as many times as I've seen Cammy do it, it's never looked like this on her. So completely sexy. So sexual. "But then, a picture. Pretty please?"

I think this is probably the worst line of thought I've ever engaged in. Because right now, all I can think about is how okay Cammy is with the idea of having her picture taken in her underwear. And how many exciting, dirty, and depraved possibilities that could lead to.

For the right guy. Not *just a friend*. Not me.

"I think we're gonna have to talk about that later, sometime when at least a little of the blood in my body is moving toward my brain."

She nods, her legs shifting together, that poor bottom lip still getting worked over.

"What do you think, Sunshine? You still want to do this?"

That hazy sensual look in her eyes turns to worry. "You don't?"

"Jesus, woman, you're looking right at it." I run my hand over my hard-on, giving the guy a settling squeeze, hoping he'll be patient. But that look in Cammy's eyes as I do it has anything but a calming effect.

She's turned on. And the way her eyes flare when I touch myself says she didn't mind that at all.

In fact, she's still watching, looking sort of mesmerized as I slide my hand up and down my shaft another time or two.

Her breath shallows, and her nipples are so hard, my mouth is watering to get a taste of them. To find out if she's as sensitive there as she is beneath her dirty little panties.

Fuck, those panties. I can't take it anymore, I need to taste her.

I need to hear her come apart with my mouth buried between her legs. I—

She starts pulling at me, wiggling beneath me.

"Rux... mouth up here... more kissing."

Chapter 8

Rux

I climb back over her, wanting to kiss her again, not just because she doesn't get kissed enough, but because it feels so damn good. Kissing has never been like this. And all I can think is, it's the friendship balancing the freedom. Like somehow the trust and soul-deep affection I have for this woman, combined with the freedom and fun of what we're doing this one time... it's like it's acting as an accelerant making everything between us burn hotter.

That, and I love giving Cammy what she wants. Granted, it's normally not a kiss or a few hours rolling around in bed, but there is nothing as satisfying as watching the smile spread across her face when I surprise her with something she didn't expect.

So I sink into the kiss again, reveling in the feel of her hands in my hair, the bare skin of her legs sliding up mine.

And somehow we find ourselves back in that desperate place, devouring each other like we can't stop. We're rocking together, grinding like teenagers. Both in our underwear, close enough to naked that every roll and press and tease has my head ready to blow off.

I want her. I want her hard and fast, and slow and gentle. I want her on her knees while I take her from behind, I want her looking up into my eyes, I want my face buried between her legs and my name echoing off the walls. I want her a thousand more ways than those.

And while I doubt very much that it's even half as bad as I want her, Cammy wants me too.

I can feel it in the clench of her fists in my hair, the squeeze of her thighs, the way her breath breaks when we move together. And if that isn't telling enough, those curvy little legs are sliding higher up my sides, and she's nudging at my shorts.

"Take these off… Need you."

"Fuck yes."

I pull her up with me, and we're both pushing at the clothes remaining between us. I get her bra, while she frees the man of steel. Her panties are next and—Christ—I can't wait.

Reaching between our bodies, I groan, finding her slick and ready. Silky soft and desperate for my touch.

There's a moment when my control seems perilously close to gone, where having her pussy so wet for me has me ready to blow like some unschooled virgin. But no way. Not after I told her what a big hot hockey stud I was.

I don't lose my cool.

I don't lose control.

I do not struggle to abide by the golden rule… She comes first.

But with Cammy…

I press a finger inside her, stroking, exploring her body to discover all its most sensitive secrets.

"*Rux.*"

Like that one right there. That sweet spot that has her breath breaking against my lips, and her inner walls clenching tight around me.

So hot. I need more, more of my name on her lips, more of that surprised startled gasp, more of what happens when I stroke and press and play right there—

"Oh my… Right there… Just like… Rux!"

Holy hell, she's going to be the end of me.

And when she's done coming against my hand, looking up at me with those wide eyes that make me feel like I've done something so much more than what I have, I can't take it.

"Baby, I've got to get inside you."

"Yes, now, please."

"Where are your condoms?"

And that's when everything comes to a screeching halt and the man of steel dies a sad little death.

There's such despair in her eyes it would almost be funny, if it weren't so painfully tragic.

"Condoms? You don't have one?"

My brow presses against hers as we lay naked together. "Baby, I was out with *you*. Why would I need condoms?"

Our eyes hold for a beat and then we fall back on the bed together laughing until we can't breathe. Damn, I love this woman.

After a moment, she turns her head, those pretty blues meeting mine. "Maybe this is a good thing. That we stopped, you know?"

I don't want to agree, but— "Yeah, maybe." We crossed some lines tonight. Lines I'd never even considered crossing with Cammy but hadn't given a second's thought to skating past tonight. And I should probably give that some thought right there. But for now, I just want to make sure wherever we've stopped, it's on solid ground. "I mean, what kind of friend would I be if I ruined you for all other dudes? And if

you got even a taste of what I can do with this guy...
damn."

Her brows pop up and her mouth opens in a little
gape. "You didn't just say that."

Oh yeah, I did. "You'd never be the same. Hell,
the bar's set so high from my kiss alone, I'm betting it's
out of reach for most guys already."

I'm expecting her to give me shit. Cut my ego
down and walk all over it. But instead she just smiles at
me. "You might be right."

I'm not. One of these days she's going to meet
some asshole I'm going to hate and she's going to love,
and the kiss he gives her is going to wipe mine from
her memory completely.

My hand finds hers, and I brush my thumb over
the top. I figure this is one of those things I won't be
doing either, but for the next minute or two, maybe it's
okay.

Cammy

WATCHING Rux get dressed is almost as hot as
watching him get undressed. Which means I'm pretty
sure I shouldn't be watching him at all. Whatever
insanity we were swept up in has passed, and with the

"friends" train back on track, it's time to stop checking the poor guy out.

But those Superman boxer-briefs are awesome. All the better with his shirt on but still hanging open. And when he steps into his suit pants and pulls them up over those crazy powerful thighs... up so the open fly is sort of cradling what is a seriously significant package before he tucks everything back behind the zipper—

"Cammy, if you're going to watch me get dressed," he says, not actually looking at me, "you got to stop biting your lip while you do. It's fucking hot and blowing holes in the 'just friends' firewall I'm trying to reconstruct."

Heat rushing into my cheeks, I jerk straight from where I was leaning against my bedroom door, ogling my friend like a piece of meat.

Bad, Cammy!

"Sorry," I squeak out, trying to look away. Failing. I do keep my teeth locked together though, so no lip-biting. But there's an unfamiliar piece of me that's preening over the idea of a man like Rux being affected by anything I do. I need to shake it off, but considering we're less than an hour out from fooling around, I'm going to cut myself some slack.

He's fastening the buttons of his shirt, those big hands and thick fingers making quick work of the task and making me wonder how I'd never recognized the hot potential of such a simple act before.

"No biting," he says, snapping his fingers and pointing to where I'm totally biting my lip again.

My hand flies to my mouth and my eyes bug.

Rux huffs out a low chuckle, shaking his head as he walks over to me. "Yeah, it's gonna take a minute for me too." He shoves his hands deep into his pockets and smiles down at where I'm standing there all *speak-no-evil*. The corner his mouth kicks up and he drops a quick kiss at my temple. "But we'll be fine."

I nod and he flashes a wink before cutting past me toward the living room.

After a breath, I follow. I hang back, watching from across the room, hating that for the first time since we met, I don't know what to say to him and the silence feels strained.

We walk to the door and Rux stops, runs a hand through that overlong hair that felt so good between my fingers, and turns to me. The look in his eyes is one I don't really know what to make of and am not entirely sure I even want to try.

"Cammy—" he starts at the same time I say, "Thank you." We both shake our heads, then putting my hand on Rux's chest, I start again. "Thank you for tonight," I say, feeling more shy than I ever have with this man. When I look up into his eyes, it's pure affection, *pure Rux* staring back at me. "I had a really good time."

He pulls me in for one of his signature one-armed hugs, tucking me into his side and burrowing his face into the top of my head. "I think you mean really, *really* good."

This guy.

Chapter 9

Rux

I've got two coffees in my hands as I push backward in through the lobby door of Greg's building.

I texted him before the sun was up about needing to talk and he agreed. But man, I don't want to do this. Hell, it's not like I've never screwed up before. I have. Too many times to count, and while I've always felt shitty when I do wrong, I've never had anything eat at my gut the way this is.

Greg is one of my best friends. We go back. There's a trust and understanding between us, and somehow, last night, I violated it completely. And something tells me explaining the whole slippery-slope thing isn't going to cut it when we're talking about his little-sister-in-law.

Generally speaking, I'm a solid proponent of most things bro-code, but what happened between Cammy and me isn't anyone's business but ours. I want to leave it at that. End of story. Thing is, Greg and I have been butting into the girls' business forever. It's like *our thing*. We're protective guys. And for me to be with Cammy the way I was—or almost was—and not own up to it? Uncool.

Which means there's a good chance he's going to lose his shit.

I'm shifting from foot to foot, and I've got the sense the security guy has his finger hovering over speed dial for the cops, because I look so damned suspect standing here waiting.

The elevator doors open, and Greg comes out wearing the coat he got the same day I got mine. Custom jobs to accommodate a wingspan that's not exactly standard.

"Ready for our day-date, girlfriend?" he asks with a gleam in his eye and a smile I'm guessing is about three and half minutes from being wiped off his face for good. At least as far as I'm concerned.

"Yeah, man," I say handing off his coffee as we head out onto the streets. I should have gotten him a cookie or something. Maybe a brownie or cake pop. Fuck.

Greg looks down the block and mutters a curse. "Jesus, that guy."

I follow his glare and sure as shit, that reporter Waters is staked out down the block. "Dude drives a Smart car?"

Everyone knows what a hard-on the guy has for our captain. *Loves him.* It's not mutual. Couple years back Waters made some unflattering comments about Julia, probably thinking they wouldn't get back to her husband. They did. And Waters has been on his shit list since, not that he knows it.

The driver's side door nearly gets taken off when he opens it into traffic. Waters ducks, putting his hands up in embarrassed surrender. Then rolls into this series of animated hand signals with some seriously mean-ingful looks toward us.

"What's he saying?"

Greg heaves a breath and gives him a sharp shake of his head. "Fuck if I know. Whatever it is, the answer is no."

The reporter's eyes bug, a sheepish smile on his face as he climbs back into his micro car. "He's not going to follow us?"

The conversation I'm about to have is the kind of

private better suited to a conversation behind doors, but there's a solid chance when Greg hears what I did, shoulder injury or no shoulder injury, he's gonna throw down. I would. And if that's how it goes, I owe it to him and Julia to make sure it doesn't happen inside their place.

"Nah. We already saw him, so he won't try any of that accidentally-running-into-us shit. A few weeks back there would have been a group of 'em parked outside looking for a bite on my status. But with no news, they've moved on. Most of them anyway."

We shoot the shit for a couple of blocks, before cutting across to the lakefront. One of the nice things about being a hockey player is that even in temps below freezing, we're acclimated enough to the cold that walking the paths in this weather is no big deal. In fact, it's kind of a treat, since most anybody else out here is gonna be bundled up, just trying to knock out their run or make their steps, and not paying much attention to the two guys out for a stroll ahead of them.

I turn to my buddy. "Hold up a minute. I've been meaning to tell you something, and I want to do it here."

His brows go up, pulling the corner of his mouth along for the ride.

"You about to pop the question, big man? Because

I like you a lot, but *as a friend*. My dick belongs to Julia, fucker."

Funny guy. I rub my jaw. That's about as good of an intro as I'm going to get.

"So speaking of friends and dicks," I start, then hearing what I just said, mutter a few choice words before trying again. "Dude, I messed up… Only I don't really feel like I did. I mean I feel bad about one part, but not the rest. Although maybe I should feel bad about the rest too. It just seemed so right and simple and straightforward at the time. And honestly you were the last thing I was thinking about, which maybe makes me an asshole, but then, if I was thinking about you at the time, maybe that would make me something else… I don't know." Shaking my head, I take a painful breath. "Fuck it, man, just lay me out. I'm ready for it. Don't worry about the teeth, but maybe stay away from the nose. I've seen you swing that sledgehammer before, and I don't think the team needs a broken nose slowing me down when we're up against the Lightning tonight. I'm serious, bring it. I deserve it."

Greg takes a sip of his coffee. "This about Cammy?"

For fuck's sake. "Yes, it's about Cammy. I just told you. Who else would it be about?"

And why is he giving me that jolly fucking smile

when I've just confessed to getting up to some seriously dirty shit with his little-sister-in-law?

He starts walking again, waving for me to follow.

"For one, you didn't tell me jack shit. You started rambling about dicks and assholes. I was thinking maybe it was just another Saturday until the whole *laying you out* business. For two, why the hell would I lay you out? Cammy's a grown woman and you're the most stand-up guy I know. We've already been buddies and teammates, there's no one else I'd rather call... *brother-in-law*."

I'm nodding, doing my damnedest to let his words sink in before I reply, but that last thing...

All forward motion ceases as a weird pressure builds in my chest, stopping my heart and making my lungs constrict as I sputter.

"Dude," I barely choke out. "You've got the wrong idea, man. This is what I was trying to tell you. It's not like that. We're friends. *Just* friends. I guess I mean not *just* just friends but mostly just friends who have this thing that we're doing, but in a friendly kind of way." Enough that I'd want way better than me for her. "Dammit, man, why are you laughing? I'm standing still. You can just hit me. Just don't fuck up your shoulder any worse."

And then Greg is doubled over a few feet in front

of me, he looks back over his shoulder, honest-to-fuck tears streaming down his face.

"You fucking *fucker*. You knew already!" He's lucky I don't lay *him* out.

Straightening to his full height, he shakes his head at the sky. "Of course, I fucking knew."

Oh. "Cammy called Julia?"

Jesus, it's barely seven. The sun's not even up.

"Uhh, yeah, I'm guessing she was on the phone before you even left her place."

Now that I think about it, she did have her phone in her hand when I was leaving.

"FYI, you owe me a full night of sleep. She called Julia and then Julia called me at four a.m. with all the squeals and breathless gossip until I was wide awake. And where the hell is my cookie? I lost five bucks to Julia thinking you'd show up with half a bakery trying to woo me back into lovin' you."

Knew I should have brought a cookie.

"Five bucks? Cheap fucker."

"Dude, you know what it's like betting against her. I had to bring the dollars down."

And like that, the tension in my chest unravels, letting me draw a couple lungs' worth of the brisk lake air. "Seriously, you're not pissed?"

"Nah, man. If it were Diesel or Bowie trying to get

under Cammy's skirt, then yeah, I'd probably have something to say about it. But you guys are friends, and so long as you're on the same page, Cammy could use some fun."

Right. "If there's one thing I'm good for—besides backing your ass up on the ice, that is—it's fun. Hell, I wouldn't have been opposed to Cammy using me for some more of it, but she was probably right about it being a good idea we stopped when we did."

"Can't believe you weren't packin'. What the hell, man?"

I shrug, not interested in explaining all the reasons random hookups have lost their appeal this year.

When he sees I'm not going to answer, he shakes his head. "So that's it with Cammy, huh? Not-quite-one-and-done? You two back to *just* friends."

"Yep." I don't hesitate. Cammy made it pretty clear where she stood last night and I get it. I mean, yeah, I've pretty much got the sounds of her coming apart for me on permanent replay in my mind and I've basically given up on talking my dick down each time I think about her. But chalk that up to me being a guy. It will pass. Eventually. Probably. And even if it doesn't, who cares. We'll still be friends, because I wouldn't let anything get in the way of that.

Rux

THANK fuck I can sleep on the plane. After leaving Cammy's place, I was up half the night with my head swimming in the sounds of her soft moans, my dick ready to drill through my mattress. That coupled with the guilt made for some serious tossing and turning.

Talking to Greg helped. And then practice helped some more.

But I need to catch some Zs. Dropping into a row to myself, I turn on my Beats and shut out the rest of the world. Kind of wish I'd been able to see Cammy, but she had to pick up Matty and… timing.

It's not a big deal. That's what I'm telling myself, even though there's this tug in my gut that feels like it is. With what happened between us last night, I want to see her. Hug her. Hear her voice and know, *really know* that I didn't jeopardize something that's as critical to me as breathing.

Maybe I'll just check in. Casual. Fun.

Me: Can't believe you told Julia.

I wait for her to come back, watching for those three little dots.

The phone rings instead and a pressure I hadn't even realized was building releases in my chest.

"Really? You can't believe it?" she teases through the line.

Smart-mouthed thing. *Don't think about her mouth.*

"You couldn't let me talk to Greg first?" I wedge a pillow behind me and angle into the corner, a grin stretching across my face. Because she's right, I should have known she'd talk to her sister before I could get to my buddy.

"Would it really have mattered?"

"Hell, yes. Ever hear of the *bro code*? I should've been the one to tell him. What if he'd been pissed? What if he'd been lying in wait, ready to beat my ass when I got there?"

I can practically see her rolling her eyes.

"Well, was he?"

"No, but he let me make a complete fool of myself trying to explain."

That laugh. That's what I needed to hear. And because I want even more of it, I start dishing the details, reveling in every giggle and smile-laced sigh.

The plane is filling up, the cushion of empty rows between me and the next guys shrinking to where I've got to be careful with my words. Not something I generally excel at, but this is Cammy.

"Hey, we good?" I lower my voice, wishing were kicked back on her couch right now so I could look into her eyes while I asked. "You okay about everything today?"

She takes a breath and I hold mine. But I can still

hear the smile in her words when she answers. "I'm good, Rux. A little distracted. People keep asking what the smile's about and where my head is."

I rub at that spot in the center of my chest, grinning. "That so?"

"Oh my God, listen to you. Is there even room in the cabin for that ego of yours or are they going to have to put it down in the cargo hold with all the other big sticks?"

"Sunshine, if you start talking about big sticks and whether things will fit—"

"Rux!"

"*What?*" I ask, playing dumb, the way she's playing at being shocked.

For a minute I just hear her breathe. It's nice, and some jacked-up part of me wonders if she'd let me record it sometime, so I'd always have it to listen to when I need to chill out. Not sure it would even work if I knew she wasn't actually there with me. Miles away but in the same moment.

"I know this might just be another Tuesday for you—"

"It's Saturday, Sunshine."

She sighs, but it's one of those good ones. "You know what I mean. Nights like last night—I don't get a lot of those. So yeah, it's been keeping a smile on my face all day."

I sit up. "Let's get something straight, last night wasn't just another Tuesday or Friday or any other day for me. Last night was different. Being with someone who means so much to me was special. And for the record, I've been getting shit for the smile on my face most of the day too."

"Really?" she asks, and damn, I wonder how it's possible she can know me so well in so many ways and not know this.

"Yeah, really." And since we're being honest, I tell her the rest. "As much as I wish I was there right now, it's probably better I'm not."

"Why's that?"

"Because it was so good, I'm having a little trouble *thinking* like a friend today. And if I was back there—" Close enough to touch. To reach out. To see if I could get her to make those same sexy-as-sin noises for me again. To see if I could get her to make them louder. "I might have trouble *acting* like one too."

She pauses, but I trust her not to freak out. Then, "Yeah, probably better then... Because you wouldn't be the only one."

I'm not the type to be at a loss for words, but that quiet admission has me stunned. I'm the jackass with impulse control issues. Not Cammy.

She's a rock. Solid. Steady. The kind of woman willing and capable of making the tough choice no matter what it costs her in order to do the right thing. And she isn't sure she'd be able to resist *me*?

"Sunshine," I half groan, trying like hell not to revisit the details of last night, but unable to fight the mental highlights reel rolling through my mind.

"I know, right?" Another soft breath, only this one doesn't calm me. It makes me think about the way her breath felt against my neck when I heard it last night. Fuuuck.

"So the road trip is a good thing. And when I get back, we'll be back on track."

"Absolutely."

"Just two good friends with one hot night between them." Shit, we're ready to take off. "Hey, I hate to say it, but I gotta go."

She wishes me a good game and we hang up. I'm about to power down the phone when I see her text come through.

Cammy: I think you meant one SUPER hot night behind us.

And the next second an attachment pops up… and holy hell, I can't believe she did it. But there, splashed across the screen I'm shielding with my hand and angling toward my chest, is the photo I took with her phone last night before I left.

It's the two of us on her bed, her bare leg thrown

over mine, Wonder Woman and Superman skivvies on proud display.

Cammy put on a tank top, but it's so thin, *fuck me*, even in this arm's-length selfie I can still see the dusky outline of her tight nipples. The tank is bunched just a little, the bottom riding around her ribs, showing off a generous stretch of smooth bare skin below.

I swallow hard.

She's looking at me in the shot, and we're laughing. Easy and happy, and this picture is so perfect, there's a part of me that knows I ought to delete it now. Get rid of it before it has a chance to dig in any deeper and seed any more of the ideas I'm not supposed to get about Cammy Wesley.

Chapter 10

Cammy

There was a time when having Jeremy calling me would have left me breathless and bursting with joy. But that feels like a lifetime ago. Today, it's mostly embarrassment as I drag myself out of the fog of a dirty dream that was just getting good. Dream Rux made another appearance last night, but he wasn't pulling that same teasing bullshit from the first time. I'd just gotten into his pants when the phone rang.

"Sorry to call so early on a Sunday," Jeremy starts tentatively as I squint at the clock.

"It's okay. I can't actually believe Matty let me sleep past seven anyway." Pushing my hair back from my face, I'm headed toward his room when I hear the clank of silverware coming from the kitchen and turn around. "What's going on?"

"Friend of mine at work has some tickets to the Museum of Science and Industry and can't use them. I know it's not my day, but I thought if you guys didn't have other plans, maybe we could all go together."

My stomach tenses. Being around Jeremy dredges up so many feelings. Honestly, I'm not sure I'm up for it.

"Oh, um. We had a few errands…" In the kitchen, I rub my hand over Matty's back and drop a kiss on his head when he leans into me. This boy has missed so much time with his dad, I don't want to be the reason he misses more.

Clearing my throat, I shake my head. "But sure. Why not."

"Great! Awesome. I'll pick you guys up about eleven."

Matty's watching me with hopeful eyes, no doubt having heard his dad through the line. "Dad's coming over today?"

And like that, whatever doubts I had about saying yes are gone.

We get a few chores taken care of before riding over all together. The museum is amazing. Matty's been there before, but it's clear being with his dad has him seeing it with new eyes. Jeremy buys us lunch and seems completely engrossed in everything Matty has to tell him, only breaking eye contact with our boy long enough to look up at me. Like I don't already know how incredible this kid's brain is.

We stay through the afternoon and by the time we leave, I'm too wiped to take Jeremy up on his offer to help with our errands. I've missed a text from Julia with a video of Rux dancing in the weight room at the hotel.

Julia: Check out what Popov sent to Greg from this morning. Rux has the moves like Jagger.

He's got something. He's pulling out the sprinkler, running man, lawnmower and Cabbage Patch that I can identify. There's a whole lot more going on I can't.

That thick hair is pulled back on top with an elastic and his face and bare chest are ruddy and glistening with sweat. And the way his abs flex and shift with each ridiculous move... Do his shorts always hang that low? How have I never noticed?

"What's that face about?" Jeremy asks from the driver's seat.

I'm about to tell him it's nothing when Matty chirps in from the back. "Is that Rux? Can I see?"

Cheeks flaming, I pull the phone to my chest, but at second glance I realize the only thing inappropriate about the video is how I'm reacting to it. With a shake of my head, I hold it up between the seats. Matty's full belly laughs have my heart ready to burst.

"Hey, feel like I'm missing out," Jeremy says, and Matty tries to describe what Rux is doing, but then just falls into a more general fanboy accounting of all things Ruxton Meyers.

And I have to give Jeremy credit, he listens, making all the appropriate noises as Matty talks about Rux showing him how to hold his stick and how for Halloween Rux showed up dressed as a pro-wrestler.

By the time Matty comes up for air, we're nearly home. Cutting a glance to Jeremy, I tease, "Bet you're glad you asked, huh?"

He considers before answering. "Yeah. Sounds like some guy. I know I've missed—" He looks away and starts again. "I want to know about the people in your lives."

I don't really know what to say, so I just nod. I mean, yeah, I'd want to know who was a part of Jeremy's life if they were going to be involved in Matty's too.

We pull up to the curb and Matty unbuckles in a flash. He thanks his dad and wraps a little arm around the front seat for a hug before zipping into the lobby where Ray is working the security desk. Jeremy gets out with me, walking around to the trunk to retrieve the poster we got from the gift shop.

"Thank you for today," I say, meaning it. "Matty had a great time and it was really nice."

He closes the trunk and turns to me with his hand resting on the metal. "So, Rux."

"Rux?"

"I didn't think you guys were really together at first. I mean Matty said you were best friends and when I googled before I came back to Chicago"—at my raised brows, he shrugs—"I didn't find any mention of you guys together… romantically, anyway."

"You asked Matty?" I'm not crazy about him talking to my seven-year-old about my love life.

His hands come up between us. "Barely. Matty was going on about Rux and I asked if he was your boyfriend. *Once*. He told me you guys were 'besties.'"

Matty is such a mimic.

Jeremy takes a breath, watching me. "It's none of my business, but are you guys—"

"Mom," Matty calls, leaning out the lobby doors, his feet doing a quick shuffle. "I gotta *go*."

I've never been more grateful for Matty's walnut-sized bladder. Sure, I liked the idea of looking like I was in a relationship with Rux, but for some reason, what happened this week has me not wanting to address it at all. I don't want to say that we're involved when I'm having a hard enough time keeping my thoughts out of his breezers as it is.

I turn back to Jeremy, but he's already climbing back in the car. "It's okay. Talk to you this week."

Cammy

IT'S an early game against the Jets, and Matty and I watch the whole thing together. He can barely keep his eyes open at the end, and when the Slayers have a 3-2 win under their belt, my kiddo staggers back to his bed for the quickest tuck-in in history.

Julia texts with me a few times and I catch up on some email. But through it all, I'm waiting to hear from Rux. When I do, I'm tucked into a corner of the couch and he's in a hotel room in New York and not on a plane heading home.

"They'll get it fixed overnight and we'll be ready to take off early," he tells me. There's a dull thud and I imagine his duffle bag landing on some nondescript desk. A clank tells me he's hung up his suit jacket.

I can see him in my mind, tugging his tie free, undoing the buttons down his shirt. Losing his belt… Opening his fly.

Stop.

We talk about the museum a little. Matty's favorite exhibits. Mine. His. The game schedule coming up. How Bowie and Static almost got into it over some girl the night before, but then neither of them ended up taking her home.

"I don't know those guys that well, but Julia says they're a handful."

"Yeah, kind of. Those defensive players spend a lot more time together than with us, but still… Yeah… So, what's on today's panties?"

I cough, grateful I've already finished my tea. "Excuse me?"

"Come on," he says, totally unrepentant. "It's just a friendly question. Innocent."

"Innocent?" There isn't an innocent bone in Rux's body.

"Mostly innocent. After 'apply within,' no way I wasn't going to ask. Especially with that picture burning a hole in my pocket the last two days."

I can feel my smile stretching wider. "So I'm not the only one mildly obsessed with that picture?"

He *hmm*s and I can all but see him stretched out in bed, that naughty smirk at full tilt.

"Cammy, I about choked on my tongue when it popped up on the plane. And all I wanted to do was stare at the damn thing the whole weekend, but I seriously would have had to put my fist into someone's face if they'd seen you like that... even accidentally."

"You are such a sweetheart. But no punching teammates."

"Yeah, I know. Hence the whole burning-a-hole-in-my-pocket thing."

"I had to bury it in a folder so it didn't just pop up if someone young and impressionable happened to open my phone." But yeah, I'm looking at it now.

"Smart."

"Rux, from one friend to another... Your body is crazy. I can't believe they don't have you doing underwear shoots."

"Had an offer, but I'm a private guy."

At this I cough. "You are not. You have no shame. You're the biggest goof I know."

"Sure, but that's with my friends. On my terms. Didn't like the idea of someone else being in charge of how much of me was out there."

"I get it. Do you mind that I have this picture? I can totally delete it." It would break my heart, but I absolutely would.

"What, don't talk crazy. I love that you have this picture." He groans and from the sound of it, I know he's looking at it now too. "That *we* do. And I can't tell you how much better I feel about you ogling my wicked ripped abs since I've been rocking a semi every time I even think about your golden lasso."

"Shut up," I say with a grin, but just the thought is enough to have that now-familiar heat churning low in my belly and my legs pressing together.

"About the panties." No way he was going to drop it. "What do they say today? 'Wrong way' across the ass? 'Slippery when wet'? More superheroes?"

I can't even believe I'm doing this, but I inch down my leggings to peek at whatever I put on this morning. Rolling my eyes, I sigh.

I shouldn't.

"I hear you debating over there. Just tell me. Or you could snap another picture. That would be totally okay too."

"Rux!"

"*Tell*," he urges, his voice lower, with shades of bedroom I've never paid attention to before.

I mumble my answer, burying my face in my hands even though he can't see me.

"What was that?" he coughs out. "I could swear you said, 'happy meal.'"

"They were from a bachelorette party! And I swear most of my panties don't say stuff like that. The ones from yesterday had Tinkerbell on them."

"Tink? Damn, that's weirdly hot. Also, not sure I believe you. May have to take a tour of the panty drawer when I get back tomorrow. Eleven work for you?"

My cheeks are starting to hurt from how hard I'm smiling. "Straight from the airport, huh."

"Hell, yes." God, he's giving me that low rumbly voice again. "And would I be right to assume I'll get to meet the much-revered *Bob* during this tour?"

I gasp, but it's mostly laugh. "You would be wrong. Bob lives in the back of my nightstand."

A sort of strangled sound comes through the line. "Cammy, you can't tell me that. You tell me '*no*' and call me a perv."

"What? You brought him up!"

"Yeah, but then you told me where he *lives*. And now I'm going to be thinking about it. And I really shouldn't be thinking about how *very close* to your bed he is. How *easy* it would be for you to roll over and get him." His voice goes even lower, all traces of that joking tone gone. "What you'd do with him."

I swallow, hard. My belly is tight. I should change the subject, but my mind is suddenly empty of anything but Rux thinking about me like that. God, it's making me hot.

"Fuck, just this once... and I won't ask again... after I left, *did you?*"

I open my mouth, but Rux cuts me off with a sharp, "No! Don't tell me. Don't tell me. I don't want to know. Double fuck, you know I want to know. But Sunshine, I think we're in agreement it's better I don't, right?"

"Rux?"

"*Cammy*." He sounds tortured. And I feel that one word all the way through me.

"Bob and I are on a break," I say, even though I know it's a mistake.

Another lower groan. "Tell me why."

"I think you know why."

His voice is so low, the rough scrape of it is almost enough to get me *there* without any assist at all. "Say it."

I'm playing with fire. But I can't stop myself from giving him the truth. "Because after what happened with us, it wouldn't be enough. And I'm not ready to let go of what we did yet."

Chapter 11

Rux

$\mathcal{I}$ thought about going home. Told myself I could use the rest after flying out of New York hours before dawn. That I should wait until Matty gets home from school and go over then. But somehow, I end up back at Cammy's place, a sort of electric charge running beneath my skin as I wait for her to open the door.

And yeah, I'm being weird with the waiting thing. Not my style. I've got a key and I'm not shy about using it. But today, knocking seems like the way to go just in case *she's* feeling weird or embarrassed or any of the other shit I hope to hell she isn't feeling.

That conversation last night wasn't what it should have been.

Yeah, we joked and caught up, but just the sound of her voice had me half hard. And that was *before* I broke every rule I'd set for myself and started working for details I knew better than to think were mine.

Like about Bob.

So much for the road trip giving me time to get back on track. I'm not sure my brain will ever work right around this girl again.

Not that I'll let on.

No way. We're friends. The best kind. And I'm not going to let a few errant boners get in the way of something that means more to me than just about anything on this planet.

So while I might be dying thinking about what her panties say today... I won't ask.

I won't.

The door opens and the breath I've been holding whooshes out. *That smile.*

"Knocking?" she asks, leaning into the open door, those lush lips set at a slant that—man, yeah—really works for me.

I try with the whole "eyes up here" business, but damn, she's wearing this cropped little sweater with jeans, and the way she's standing leaves about an inch of bare skin exposed on one side.

"Rux?"

My eyes snap up and guilt swamps me.

Friends, fucker.

"Hey, Cammy." Dropping a kiss at her temple, I step around her into the apartment, trying not to look at that spot next to the door or think about how deep my fingers were inside her last time I was here. Trying not to think about how wet and tight she was. Those desperate little sounds she made.

Damn.

"Did you come straight from the airport?" she asks, following me in.

"Yeah, I thought…" Shit, I don't even know what I was thinking. And worse, now that I'm back in her place, it's like I've never been here before. I don't know where to go. Where to sit or stand.

Every spot seems rife with untapped sexual potential. The couch, yeah, I want to punch myself in the face for what I'm thinking when I look at it. The kitchen table, where I've sat with her and Matty so many times, I'm mentally defiling with images of Cammy sitting on the edge, bare legs spread while I devour her *happy meal.* The fridge, I'd back her up against it, fill her with hard thrusts. I could sit on the overstuffed chair—it's built for one, but it would be so easy to tuck a finger into the pocket of those sexy jeans and tug her in until she straddled my lap.

No matter where I sit it's going to feel like I'm putting some damn move on her.

That's it. I need to leave.

Turning to tell her I'll be back when Matty gets home, I stop short when I catch those big blues jumping back to mine, looking *so guilty*.

So hot.

What was I going to say?

Her teeth sink into the flesh of that lush bottom lip, her eyes dipping to my mouth. Lingering there long enough I can almost taste her kiss again. Christ, I want to taste her again.

"Cammy," I choke out, fighting the muscles that are straining to reach out and touch.

"You're not looking at me like a friend," she says, and *fuuuck*, the way she says it—a little breathless—isn't helping.

"Maybe the road trip wasn't long enough." Or maybe I shouldn't have asked about Bob or what her panties looked like.

And then I'm staring at the fly of her jeans, wondering what's underneath.

Don't ask.

"Hearts."

"Huh?" *Stop staring, man.*

Only how the hell am I supposed to stop when her hands are sliding over her hips, her thumbs skimming beneath the waist.

I gulp watching the denim inch lower on one side,

lower. Low enough to expose the fitted white cotton patterned with tiny red hearts.

And then it's *my* hand reaching out, my fingers skimming over the waist of her jeans before hooking over the brass button. My knuckles grazing the baby-soft skin below her navel as I tug her closer.

And it's her fingers skimming light over my fore-arms to where my shirt is rolled at the cuffs. Her hands smoothing across my chest, dropping lower and then pushing up, up. High enough to slip around the back of my neck.

What is it about feeling her fingers linked like that?

There aren't a lot of ways to read this. If the girl in my arms was some bunny from two years ago, I'd already be looking for a private space. But this isn't a bunny. It's Cammy who dreams of happily ever afters and the kind of forever I couldn't live with ruining. And so even though I'm starting to sweat from holding myself back, I keep fucking doing it.

Ducking my head, I look into her eyes. "Cammy, this isn't what you want." Is it?

"What if I want you to keep looking at me exactly like you are?"

Damn it. Don't ask. "How am I looking at you?"

The pink tip of her tongue touches her bottom lip. "Like you want to finish what we started as bad as I do."

I can't breathe, can't form words. I need to let her go, only instead of setting her back, my fists ball in the sides of her jeans.

"Just once," I manage. It won't be enough. I know it, like I know how to breathe. But I don't care. I meant what I said, I'll give her anything.

Her eyes break from mine, following her hands back down my chest to where she starts playing with the luckiest button in all the land. "Or I mean, maybe more than once?"

My heart stops beating, then starts again, pumping at double time. Filling my chest with something so fucking good.

"I mean, I'm not asking you to be my *real* boyfriend. I know that's not—it's not what either of us want from each other. But maybe, since there's this thing between us. And we've already crossed the line. Maybe for a while, we could just... have some fun together."

"Some fun?" I ask, my fingers hooking in the front of her jeans as I pull her closer.

Her eyes flare and then go hazy, telling me she doesn't mind my caveman slipping his leash, just a little.

"For a while. Not forever. I promise. I mean, so long as we're careful around Matty."

I nod. "So instead of going back to being *just*

friends, maybe we have some fun being *more than* friends." She knows how I feel. Where my lines are drawn. Jesus, could we really do that? "For how long?"

She shakes her head. "For however long it feels right."

I think about the way she came apart for me the last time I was here, the sounds she made. And I'm pretty sure I can keep her feeling right forever.

Not forever. Cammy's too smart to invest that beautiful heart in a man she knows can't give her the future she wants. And I know myself. I care about her too much to even want her to try.

"For however long it feels good," I agree, moving my hands back to her hips and sliding them down and around below her ass. I pick her up and start toward the bedroom. "Starting now."

Cammy

RUX'S HANDS ARE EVERYWHERE. Cradling my face, gripping my ass, racing over my body like he can't decide what he wants to touch first. How he wants to hold me. Touch me.

And I'm the same. I don't know where to start or

stop with him. Heck, that's not true. I don't want to stop with him at all.

I want it all. I want every bit of him I can get and I want it all now.

We haven't set a time limit on what we're doing, but it's not going to last forever. There's a limit on this, and God, I want to make the most of every minute.

So yeah, my hands are racing up his body, bunching in his hair, fanning out over his cheeks as we devour each other.

He picks me up, holding me against him with one arm banded around my lower back and the other below my ass.

"I have condoms," I gasp against his lips.

"Good, I only have three in my wallet."

Three?

"Matty gets home from school at quarter to four."

"That's five hours from now. How many did you buy?"

"Ten?"

"Nice, we probably shouldn't have to go out for more, then."

He's joking. I'm sure he's joking.

Isn't he?

My back meets the mattress and then Rux is on top of me, pulling me farther up the bed with the strength of that one arm behind me.

Wow.

And then we're rolling together, kissing and touching, sighing and gasping. Pulling at each other's clothes like neither one of us can believe we'll get another chance at this.

Like at any second, it might end.

Like we're starving for each other.

His mouth moving over my neck and chest like he can't get enough. My knee slides higher, my hips shifting restlessly beneath him until he slots his other leg between mine, bringing us into alignment.

I moan my relief when he draws back and then rocks forward, dragging the thick ridge of his cock over me just right.

It's so good. So hot, when he straightens his arms and, bracing above me, watches as he does it again and again.

Everything inside me is winding tight, ramping higher, but I don't want to get off like a teenager in the back of a car. "I want you inside me."

His eyes close, head dropping between his shoulders before coming back up.

"*Sunshine.*"

And then he's back down the bed, dropping wet, openmouthed kisses along the way. I arch up to undo my bra, and the sound Rux makes has me clenching hard around the space that aches to be filled. He works my jeans down my legs and whips his shirt overhead and shucks his own jeans and underwear after tossing a square foil packet toward the top of the bed. Coming back up for the heart-covered panties partially responsible for getting us here in the first place, he presses a kiss above my sex and nuzzles his nose into the cotton before slipping them down my legs.

He starts prowling his way back up. More kisses, more hungry growls.

I know where he's going as he licks and bites his way up my inner thighs, getting closer and closer to where I need him most.

But not like that.

Catching his hair between my fingers, I nudge him higher.

"Like this, I can't wait."

His eyes meet mine and hold. A nod. He makes fast work of the condom, rolling it on.

"Wait." My hand moves to the center of his chest. "Is that as far up as it goes?"

Rux looks down at himself, then back at me. And the smile on his face is pure Rux and makes me hotter than I've ever been.

"It's on all the way."

"It's safe like that?" I mean, I want this. But one unplanned baby is enough for me.

He nods. No teasing. His hand runs up his length

and more liquid heat spills through my center at the sight.

Wow.

Slipping his fingers between my legs, he strokes. "So wet for me." He presses one finger inside and I rock up into the touch. It's so good, but I want more.

He gives me another finger, pushing in again, stretching me in ways I know won't compete with him.

"I want to feel you inside me. I need it, Rux."

His mouth meets mine and he lines up, positioning himself at my opening. He's so much bigger than his fingers.

"I'll go slow," he says, breaching my body with the heavy length of his cock.

"Rux," I gasp, my breath stalling in my chest, my eyes going wide with shock.

He's big. Bigger than anyone I've ever been with. Not that there have been a lot. But it's different.

The pressure is intense, stealing my breath as Rux eases in then back, giving me a taste of what's to come but not all at once. Letting me adjust to the way he's stretching me beyond what I'd thought my body could take and then taking it away... so by the time he gives it back, I'm desperate for it.

"You're so— *Oh God*."

He eases off. "Too much?"

I shake my head, pulling my heel up the back of his thigh, like I could somehow hold him in place. "No. Or yes? *Don't stop.*"

That smile. That smile kills me.

He's still easing in and out, still teasing me just like in my dreams.

"You want my cock? You want to feel me so deep inside, you don't know where I stop and you begin?"

He licks into my mouth, his tongue slick against mine. "You want me to give you all you can take, and then give you more?"

"Yes. Rux, yes!"

He's deeper now, and God I can barely breathe with the way he's filling me. My hands are everywhere. His shoulders, his back. His hair, gliding across his jaw and then caught in the gentle clasp of his teeth as he finds the deepest place inside me and holds.

"There," I gasp, my body spasming around the stretch and strain of him so big within me.

"Here?"

Clenching and hugging like it wants more.

"*Please.*"

"Anything you want, Sunshine." And he pushes in again, long and deep, butting up against the limit of what I can take.

"Fuck, you're so tight. Don't want to hurt you."

"So good," I pant, desperate for more. "Not hurting me."

This man could never hurt me.

"Harder." I want to feel him for days.

He gives me what I ask for, watching me with eyes that track everything. "You like that?"

"So much."

"You want me to make you come?"

"Yes!"

He leans down and kisses me again, deep and dirty and so freaking good.

"You get this first one easy, because I'm going to die if I don't feel you coming all over my cock. But then you're going to have to work for the next one. Okay?"

I'm nodding, frantic. Because he could probably ask me to sign over my bank account to him and if I thought he was going to take me there, I'd do it.

And then he's sliding in and out, hitting that spot with every thrust, making my breath catch and my body shatter.

When my muscles go lax, he slows his movements and leans down to kiss me again. He makes love to my mouth, and it's so sweet, so thorough, so good that, already, I'm winding tight again.

Already arching into him.

Sliding my heels up so they lock behind his back.

I want more.

"You ready?" he asks, slowly rocking his hips into me.

"Yesss. So ready."

"Then hold on."

Chapter 12

Cammy

"So you saw him yesterday and it was totally normal. Like just *friends* friends?" Julia asks two days later, clutching her beer to her chest as fans filter around us finding their seats in the arena.

"Yeah. But we agreed Matty wouldn't see anything change between us. So even if my heart starts to skip when Rux walks in, there's no kissing or flirty fooling around in front of impressionable children who might get the wrong idea."

"Yeah but Matty is always darting off for something. Rux didn't do one of those accidentally-on-purpose stunts where he drags his knuckles along the outside of your boob when you get thirty seconds alone?"

My face scrunches up. "Is that one of his signature moves or something?"

"No. But... I mean, if you guys are going for the full benefits package, it seems like maybe you ought to be getting more benefits, is all."

I shake my head trying not to get too caught up in thoughts of how many benefits I've enjoyed already.

So many.

So good.

I take a steadying breath. "I'm pretty confident I'll be getting more of Rux's *package*. But the stuff with Matty is pretty important to me. And it actually means a lot to me that it's important to Rux too. He gets it. We're going to be friends no matter what. And while what we're doing is really, really fun for us... it's not really fair to put something in front of Matty that isn't going to be there permanently."

She nods and takes a sip of her beer. Then another.

"But not even one little kiss when Matty is in the other room?"

"Just the same little peck on the top of my head I've been getting since about the second night we met."

Another nod. Another swallow.

"So does that mean you guys aren't going to be all over each other after the game?"

I don't really know what to expect after the game. "Honestly, I kind of think it's going to be business as usual while we're out. I mean, we didn't nail down a schedule or ink out a contract. I think it's just... on the table. So maybe once in a while... but who knows."

"But Matty's at Jeremy's tonight. So after?"

"Yeah, after."

Her smile stretches wide and I shake my head. "Julia, seriously, don't get any ideas. This thing with us is just about having some fun."

"Um, this thing with Greg and I was just about some fun too."

That's how it started for them. A decade-old IOU for a single kiss. Just some fun between old friends. But there was one significant difference. "You might have just been having some fun, but I'm pretty sure Greg was in it for real from the start." She gets that dreamy smile on her face that makes me believe in happily ever afters. "Thing is, it's not like that with Rux. And it's not like that with me either."

Her shoulders droop and she looks over at me. "Why not? He's such a good guy."

"Julia, I know what a good guy he is. I love him like crazy and he's one of my best friends. But Rux isn't looking to settle down. He's really upfront about it. And while I want this with Rux right now, the guy has told me flat-out he's not good at being in a relationship. He doesn't want kids. He's a loyal friend and a solid teammate, but I don't want to mess things up between us by trying to make this into something it can't be."

She slumps in her seat, but she doesn't say anything more. Because she knows I'm right.

It's like the very first thing you learn about him. And usually he's told you himself.

The music in the arena is pumping, the seats around us filling up. I look over at my sister as the Slayers come onto the ice to warm up.

I wait for Rux to hit the ice and cheer as he skates by giving us a grin as he raps the glass and leaves me just a little breathless.

The game is fast paced and intense. Rux ends up in the box in the second and finishes the game with two assists. Julia and I end up on the big screen a few times, which I've gotten used to since her career took off. When the final buzzer sounds, we've won and I'm a little hoarse from all the cheering and laughing with my sister.

Julia checks her phone and looks up toward the owners' box where Greg gives her a wave.

"Okay, he's going to hang back with the guys and meet us over at the Five Hole later."

I give him a wave too and then shoot Rux a quick text congratulating him on the game while a couple kids wearing Baxter jerseys come up to say hi to Julia and give her a note to pass to her husband.

After, we make our way over to the bar with what feels like half the arena. Everyone's pumped from the win, talking about the game, but I'm quiet, my thoughts revolving around a certain player and what my chances are of scoring with him tonight.

I'm sure we said more than once. But I don't want to make any assumptions.

I mean, we might not be in the same place. Rux hasn't suffered any shortage of available and willing gorgeous women... Cripes, I suddenly don't want to think about that at all.

Julia and I find Nat and George in back and join them at their table.

"I'm just saying, a big wedding isn't really my thing," Nat hedges. "Not that I don't want one at all."

George nods, then looks to Julia. "You went through this a couple years back. Think small is even possible with this team?"

I snicker, remembering Julia sweating over the plans, and tease, "Have you gotten enough distance from the trauma of that guest list to be able to talk about this, sis, or do you need another year or so?"

Julia snorts over her beer and shoots me an evil glare before answering. "I think you can do anything you want. You just have to have a really clear idea of what that is. If you're not entirely firm, you're going to end up with a list a million people long and... it can get overwhelming. That said, once the planning was done, my wedding kicked ass."

Nat and I agree. And then we're going through pictures on our phones to show George. Brainstorming about wedding favors and catching up on Quinn O'Brian's latest unsuccessful effort to secure George's Dad's approval to marry his daughter.

"You can never, ever, tell Greg this," Julia says, waving us all in over the table to hear whatever dirty secret she's about to reveal, though I'm pretty sure I know what it is.

"Spill," Nat says, eyes gleaming. Nothing makes her day more than having something over her brother.

Julia takes a dramatic breath and then confesses in a rush, "My childhood dream wedding happened on the fifty-yard line at Soldier Field."

Yep, that's the one.

Natalie actually blanches, while George's head spins back and forth, like she's terrified someone might have overheard. But anyone who knows Julia knows the only thing that could make her love Greg more was if he'd played football instead of hockey.

Nat reaches for Julia's hand and swears, "I'll never breathe a word."

Recovering over a slug of her beer, George elbows her buddy. "Tell yours."

"I wanted a wedding on a yacht," Nat says, her cheeks turning pink. "With the wedding party on Jet Skis at either side."

Julia's nodding, her grin wide. "Nice. Bikinis or formal wear?"

"Formal all the way," George chimes in with delight. "She confessed it after too many Jell-O shots junior year. Spilled every detail."

And those details keep piling up, until we're all cracking up so hard we don't even notice when the guys arrive until George looks up and leaps out of her chair, with Natalie quick to follow. Quinn and Vaughn catch them up in their arms, while Greg catches Julia's offered hand and leans down for a kiss. Rux is bringing up the rear and despite what I told my sister earlier, I have no idea what to expect seeing him tonight. He slants that epically sexy grin at me, grabbing a chair from the other end of the table and circling around to park it beside mine.

We always sit together, but this time watching him move into the space beside me has my belly going into freefall and a million questions about what happens once we're alone taking flight.

"Hey," I say, smiling at him like a total goof.

"Hey, yourself, Sunshine," he answers, sliding his

hand around the back of my neck and drawing me forward in a move so smooth, I don't even realize what's happening until his mouth meets mine for a kiss. A kiss that lasts. And lasts.

When he draws back, he's sitting beside me and my hand is on his chest. Our eyes are locked, his crinkling a little at the edges. "Been waiting all day for that," he says with a wink. "Guessing you didn't tell them we've joined the cutest couple competition?"

I blink and turn back toward the table, where six sets of eyes are locked on us, mouths hanging open to varying degrees.

My breath leaks out on a shaky laugh. And I'm as struck dumb as the rest of my friends.

Couple?

Rux doesn't have the same problem. "Christ, pull it together, girls," he says, pointing around the table, stopping at Quinn for a short slap followed by another direct point.

Leaning back, he drags my chair right up against his and pulls me into his side. "If you've got questions, bring 'em."

I definitely have questions. "*Rux.*"

But he just leans in and presses a quick kiss against my lips. Then another. Before nodding to Vaughn. "Go."

"Uhhh…" Vaughn eyes dart between us. "Since when?"

"Day before yesterday. It's new." Then flashing me a saucy smile, he adds, "Mostly."

George presses both hands flat on the table, gaping at me. "You're *dating* Rux and you sat here with us for over an hour without mentioning it?"

"She wanted to fire up the phone tree," Rux lies easily, giving my shoulder a squeeze, "but we decided to wait until we were all together to share the big news."

Julia snorts and Greg just looks at the ceiling.

Quinn is shaking his head, eyes narrowed. "Bullshit. This is still about The Blip, right?"

God, I'd completely forgotten the guy who inadvertently set this ball in motion. But yeah, that makes the most sense.

"Nope."

I look to Rux. "Nope?"

He shakes his head and comes in for another kiss. This one sort of stealing my breath.

When he answers, it's me he's talking to. "I can be good around Matty. But no way will I be able to keep my hands off you when he isn't around. And since you haven't hauled off and slugged me, I'm guessing you don't totally mind. But I figure if we're going to have some fun together, we should make the most of it. Go big or go home. It doesn't change what's actually happening between us or how far it's going to go. Yeah?"

I bite my lip, thinking about what he's saying. It makes sense. At least enough sense that I nod. "So I get to feel you up as much as I like?"

He grins, brushing my lip with his thumb. "Knock yourself out."

"And then we don't have to worry about dancing around lines that we can't really see. There's when we're with Matty. And when we're not."

All or nothing. I smile because it's so Rux, I don't know how I didn't see it coming.

"Okay."

"Okay." His eyes twinkle as he smiles down at me. "And FYI, you've got about another five minutes before I throw you over my shoulder and haul your fine ass out of here."

"Yeah?"

"I've been accumulating a list of the dirty things I want to do to you since I walked out of your place two days ago. Actually from before I even left."

My breath catches and heat starts to build low in my center. "Two days' worth? Sounds like quite a list."

"I've got it in Google Keep."

I blink. He's not— This is Rux. Of course, he's serious.

Chapter 13

Rux

"I'm the *master* of restraint. The king," I say against Cammy's neck, backing her into her apartment and kicking the door closed behind us.

My coat hits the floor and then hers.

"You have the patience of a toddler," she gasps as I undo her jeans with one hand and push them down her hips. She toes off her sneakers and steps out of the denim.

I lose my tie and start on the buttons of my shirt.

"I waited *days*." And I'd intended to wait until we got back here before letting myself off the leash, but one look at Cammy wrapped up in my number, cheeks pink, lips bare as she laughed with our friends, and I was done. "You're lucky I didn't rip your clothes off and do you on the table right there in front of the whole bar."

Her hands smooth up my abs and pecs, skimming over my shoulders. "*So lucky.*"

That touch.

I reach for her and she hooks one smooth leg around my waist and then the other, holding on as I cup her perfect ass and carry her back to her room. "Mm-hmm. Like a champ, I settled for a few tame kisses, a pointed and timely conversation about the state of our union—"

"You didn't even give me three of the five minutes you promised with our friends."

True. But I have an excuse. "I needed to hear you moan."

Like, on a critical, next-breath level.

It's never like this for me. Never this driving, irrepressible need to get closer, to have more. But with Cammy, I can't get enough. I can't get her out of my head and not just in that friendly, fun, *Cammy would love this* way I think about her most of the time. But in the *I'm going to fucking lose my mind if I don't get my hands on her* way.

It's not just that I know this thing between us is short term. I'm not a relationship kind of guy so they're all short term.

No, the difference is her. It's that I love this girl—

not in a put-a-ring-on-it, let-me-ruin-your-life way—but in the way that only the best friends can care about each other. Every little whimper, gasp, and broken cry I wring from her means something to me on a level that surpasses some stroke to my ego for getting her off.

It's the caring between us, the friendship, the love that has me pulling her into my lap and stealing kisses left and right.

Her legs tighten around my waist, bringing the hot, sweet spread of her into closer contact with my cock.

"We were in the bar, stud." She sighs softly and, yeah, that sound has me rocking into her as I lay her back on the bed.

"Which is why I didn't take you upstairs and fuck you right there." Christ, I wanted to so bad. That VIP party room is always empty. Filled with potential dark corners just begging to be used. So yeah, master of restraint.

"No, you just kissed me into next week."

"Next week, huh?" My hands smooth over the dip of her waist. "Sounds like it wasn't totally terrible." I know it wasn't. Her moans were so hot, I'm in danger of blowing my load right now just thinking about them.

"*Terrible?*" Her eyes go wide and then her head tips back as she gives me that gorgeous full-bodied laugh that hits me in all the best places. "When are you going to get over that? It was a *fake kiss* that I didn't see coming and I didn't even say it was terrible. You weren't even trying."

Lowering my mouth to hers, I tease her with the barest brush of contact. "No, you didn't." Another whisper of a touch. "You told Julia it was meh."

Her lips part beneath mine, and I give her my tongue. One wet stroke. Two.

She shivers, her hands fisting in my open shirt. "But you've more than made up for it."

I'm aware, but I'm not ready to stop playing. "That so?"

A nod. "Your kiss, when you put a little effort into it—"

I cut her off with another slick stroke of my tongue and a nip of her sweet bottom lip.

"—is earth-shattering. Life-affirming." Her voice drops to a whisper. "Nearly enough to make me come on its own merit."

"Nearly? Think we're gonna have to give that kiss another test drive... On a different road."

The confusion that flashes through her eyes is gone a heartbeat later when I start crawling back down her body so I can drop a kiss at the very tiny, very sexy bow on the front of her pale yellow panties. Hooking my fingers into the sides, I ease them down her curvy hips. "Lift."

I should've done this before. I'd wanted to, maybe even made a move in that direction, but we were so desperate, I can still feel the tug of her fingers in my hair, pulling me up as she demanded what she wanted.

So hot.

But now I know what I want. And it's the taste of her coming on my tongue. Her cries echoing around this apartment, my name on her lips as I prove the value of my kiss in the best possible way.

Damn.

"Rux, I see where you're going here."

"I should hope so."

Hell, I've already got one of her legs free. Christ, she's so sexy. Her pussy's bare, soft, and so wet my mouth's watering for her already. I toss her panties aside and lean in—only to have her legs shift closed as she sort of catches my face and tries to pull me up.

"Not tonight, Sunshine." I duck and weave. "It's on my list."

"I... um... Rux, you don't have to."

That's crazy talk. "Baby, my mouth is watering for a taste of you." Only then, the tension in her voice registers, sucking some blood back into my bigger head for an emergency consult. Disentangling from her gorgeous legs, I straighten my arms to look at her face. "You don't like it?"

She bites the corner of her lip and looks away. Which bothers me on a level I'm not expecting. Cammy's supposed to be able to tell me anything.

"Hey, Cammy, look at me?"

She lets out a hesitant breath. "I've never actually —I mean, I don't—" She shakes her head, giving me a pitiful look.

"Jeremy didn't do it?" That guy just gets lower in my estimation every time she tells me something new. Of course he didn't. But I'd bet dollars to donuts, he was all about the blowjobs. Selfish fucker.

"I think he would have if I'd wanted to, but I was shy. Embarrassed."

She was so damn young. And then she was pregnant.

"And none of the guys since?"

A shrug.

Jesus.

The bluest eyes meet mine. "Rux, I've only been with two other guys besides you and both were… Look, I haven't done most things."

My muscles start to lock. "I hate Jeremy."

She levels me with a look. "Don't. He gave me Matty, and I wouldn't trade that little boy for anything. Yeah, my life changed a lot when I got pregnant. And I

143

haven't done as many things as most women my age. But I have so much. I know I'm the lucky one."

Christ, she's the most beautiful woman I've ever met. Even more beautiful on the inside than she is on the outside. And that's saying a lot.

I hate it that Cammy hasn't had this. That even now when I'm offering it, she's too uncertain to accept.

"Here's the thing, Sunshine," I say, going back to my elbows so my body is resting between her legs as I look up into her face. "I think you might like it. A lot. In fact, I'm pretty sure if you let me try it, you might find that you like it so very much you'll be begging me to go down on you every time we're alone."

She rolls her eyes, but that hint of a smile is back on her lips, so I'll take it. "That confident, are you?"

"Oh yeah." And then some.

"Rux, I just—"

"Do you trust me?"

She lets out a huff of a breath, because she knows I have her. She trusts me more than any other guy she knows.

"You know I do. More than anyone, it's just—"

When she doesn't continue, I nudge. "Baby, aren't you curious what all the fuss is about? I mean, you've got girlfriends and I'm pretty sure the lot of you over-share almost as much as me. Give me a taste, and then you decide what you want."

"I'm nervous," she whispers, and my heart breaks right there.

"Have I done anything you didn't like?"

"No."

"Just a taste, Sunshine." I'm dropping kisses across her belly, swirling my tongue around those sexy hollows below her hip bones. "Say yes."

"Yes," she whispers, her voice shaky.

Taking her hands in mine, I drop a kiss to each palm and then guide them to my hair, before edging back. "You're going to want to hold on."

Her eyes go wide, but she does what I ask, sliding her fingers into my hair and gently rubbing my head as I begin to kiss her hips and thighs.

I pull one leg over my shoulder and then the other, watching her face the whole time. She's nervous, but I want her to know how good I can make her feel. And I don't want her to feel like she's missed out on anything.

I start slow, pretty confident I'm going to have all the time I want once she gets past the initial insecurities.

Using my nose, I brush along the slickness of her soft lips, one side and then the other, listening to how her breath catches and gauging the tension in her legs, how her hands stop moving altogether once I touch her. I kiss that tender, sweet skin, softly suckling here and there, flicking my tongue once, twice. Getting her used to where I am before I take what I want… A long, leisurely lick through the very center of her, ending at her clit.

"Fuck," I groan, tasting her on my tongue. "Baby, you're so sweet." Another slow lick, because I can't help myself. "So good."

Her fingers curl in my hair and another breath shudders out of her. I meet her eyes from across the expanse of her body. "Okay?"

She nods, the motion jerky and tense, her eyes hazed with need.

"Good, because I can't get enough." And then I sink into it, making out with her pussy the way I've fantasized. Deep, openmouthed kisses with tongue and teeth, her hands fisting in my hair, her hips rocking up as she begs me with her body for more. Unintelligible sounds of pleasure, hers and mine, filling the room around us.

Cupping her ass in my hands, I lift her into my kiss, bury my tongue inside and groan at the feel of her clamping down.

"Rux, oh God, please, please… *please*."

She's close, and I'm devouring her like a savage now. I can't get enough of her taste, those broken cries, and the way she's let go for me completely.

I want to give her what no one else ever has, I want

to be the one who changes how she thinks about this kind of sex. I want to be the one she can't get enough of. The one she can't let go. The one who makes her come so hard, she can't remember any other man ever getting her there but me.

"Rux!" Her thighs start to jerk as her back bows, pushing her against my mouth as she comes, writhing and panting, and it's taking everything I've got not to come against her sheets. But I want to be inside her. I want to push her over the edge again.

I keep making love to her with my mouth until she goes limp beneath me, then kiss her inner thighs before easing them from my shoulders so I can crawl up her body. Her hands are still in my hair and she pulls me in for a kiss that goes on and on. I should be frantic by now, breaking records getting a rubber on, but this feels like everything.

It's hot as fuck that she let me into her mouth with the taste of her still coating my tongue. And that little moan at the first tentative brush, then her bolder curl and slide as our mouths fuse, becoming one, has the primitive part of me hammering the cage I keep it in with one word over and over and over.

Mine.

Yeah, I could hold on to this kiss forever. I could hold on to her longer than that.

But I won't because she deserves more.

Chapter 14

Cammy

"Seriously, what's with all the recycling?" Julia asks, looking back at me over her shoulder after trying to stuff a gum wrapper in the bin overflowing with Prime packaging beneath the sink.

I can feel the heat pushing into my cheeks as I peer around the doorway to make sure Matty's not in the living room. Satisfied the coast is clear, I answer, "Rux. He's been sending me little things here and there, and this week with him on the road, maybe he's gone a little overboard."

Her brow hikes.

"It's not like that," I assure, knowing she's thinking back to when she and Greg were new, and he sent her a vibrator.

"What's he sending then?"

Another quick look and seeing that Matty is still safely occupied in his room, I open the button on my jeans and inch them down just enough to show her the panties he sent yesterday.

"Oh my God, he's sending you lingerie?" Then her eyes pop wide. "Wait, is that a picture of a *muffin*?"

"Yeah, with a little bite taken out of it. Seriously, it's so cute in this dirty Rux kind of way."

"Unconventional romantic, huh?"

That he is. And sweet and sexy and such a freaking amazing human being, I'm having to remind myself more and more that this thing with him isn't forever. The friendship is. But it's my access to this other side of him that buys me panties with a picture of his favorite snack on them that's got a ticking clock on it.

"So... are these the only panties or are those other packages from pairs with pictures of... ribs and suckers on them too?"

"There's a pair with a dandelion and the words 'blow me'. And—" I think about the ones from Valentine's Day that say, 'Rux, licked it first, so it's his' and decide against sharing the specifics. "There are a bunch. They're all kind of a blend of cute and sexy. And super comfy. No thongs."

"*Really?* I would have thought he'd be a thong guy."

"Me too, actually, and maybe he was with the other women he's been with. But with me, it's like he only buys me stuff that fits exactly who I am."

Julia's smile gets a little wobbly and she takes a deep breath. "Because you're everything he wants, just the way you are."

I nod, my smile starting to stretch out of control. For what we have now, yeah.

"So you just wear his panties and then... tell him about them when he calls?"

I'm suddenly completely engrossed in wiping up a bit of nothing from the counter. Fiddling with the cooking utensils in the pitcher by the range.

"Cammy," she whisper-gasps, and then she's the one rushing to the doorway to check that the coast is clear. "*Spill!*"

"Okay, okay, I don't *just* tell him about them. I might take a picture for him." Or even indulge in a video call, though up until last night, they hadn't escalated quite so intensely.

"You dirty girl!"

That's what he said. But with more reverence and appreciation than my sister's delighted shock.

"So, that's kind of a big deal. Or maybe it isn't," she hedges, cocking her head. "It would be for me."

"It was for me too." I move to the table where we

used to spend every night catching up when she still lived here. Sliding into my chair, I run my hand over the grain of the table. "I mean, I never would have done that with any of the other guys I dated." I wouldn't have even been tempted. "But this is Rux, and I trust him."

He hadn't even asked me to send that first picture. He'd just been giving me that deep rumbling moan, talking about how hard it got him knowing I was wearing the panties he sent me. Imagining them on me.

I liked hearing this big, hot hockey stud with so much experience in his past getting all worked up because of *me*. And I'd just done it. Taken the sexy selfie and sent it to him, never doubting that it would be safe in his hands.

Julia slides into the chair across from mine. "Does this mean things are maybe getting more serious... in a real way between you?"

"You know how you always said if a guy says he isn't good enough... I should believe him?"

"Yeah," she says warily. "But—"

"Julia, he doesn't want kids. And he told me himself, when it comes to relationships, he's not someone I could count on and he'd never want to let me down like that."

Her shoulders sag as she leans back in her chair. "I

guess that kind of straightforward warning would be pretty hard to ignore."

I nod, but I don't mention that there are times, when I'm tucked into Rux's arms while we watch some docuseries late at night, that it's easier to forget than she'd think. And when that happens, when for just a few moments, I stop reminding myself that this thing between us won't last, it feels like I could be happy forever.

"It wouldn't be fair to either of us, you know? What makes this so good, so safe, is that both of us know who we are on a fundamental level to the other."

"Friends."

"Friends." The closest of friends, having the kind of fun I would never be able to have with someone who wasn't Rux. "It's enough."

Rux

SOMETHING'S OFF TONIGHT. The locker room talk around me is more subdued than usual. Conversations happening around me in voices lower than you generally hear before a game and it's screwing with my mojo. I try rousing the guys with some tunes and trash talk, but it doesn't work and shit—I need to get my head in the right place before hitting the ice.

Checking the clock, I've still got a few minutes. I pull out my phone to call Cammy—not check out the picture she sent me last night. I'm not gonna look. That picture was hot enough to melt the ice in the arena, and no way I'm opening it with the guys from the team everywhere.

Besides, O'Brian's the guy who gets wood in the locker room thinking about his girl. Not me.

Fine, not that I've been busted for anyway, and I'd like to keep it that way.

Nah, tonight I just want to talk to her. Hear her voice. Find out what she and Matty are doing while I'm waiting to play. I want to hear whether she finished the project she's been working on for her boss at the hospital and if the shoes she ordered from Zappos were as cute as she thought they would be and what the kitchen looked like after Matty made spinach shakes for breakfast.

I want that grounding sound of her voice and her laughter soothing my soul.

Only when I head out of the locker room trying to find a spot where I've maybe got a chance at a little privacy, my call goes straight to voicemail.

I text her instead, telling her I'll talk to her later.

That I miss her.

Yeah, I'm a softy. Big surprise.

When I look up, Bowie and Kellog are waving me over from where they're parked at one of those folding tables set up for cards. I hold out my fist and bump with both the D-men, dropping into the open seat.

It's Kellog who asks, "You hear about Baxter?"

Pretty sure we all know what's coming, but, "Nah, man. What'd you hear?"

He leans in, looking around before answering. "I heard they're making an announcement after the game. He's out."

It feels like I just took a puck to the gut. I knew it was coming. But not tonight.

Though maybe I should have. I had a missed call from Greg this afternoon, but couldn't get a hold of him when I called back.

The guys nod, their faces drawn. This is what's off tonight. The weird vibe I was getting in the locker room. The reason the coaching staff has been huddled up all day.

"How'd you hear?"

"Bowie heard it from Static, who got it from that reporter he was banging last year."

"Christ."

They nod, both looking disheartened. And I get it. It sucks losing a player so central to the team. Losing our captain.

I leave the guys to it and try Baxter again. Voice-mail. I call Julia. The same.

And then Cammy even though I already called. But this time, she picks up, sounding breathless and happy. "Ooh I thought I wasn't going to get to talk to you again until after the game!"

"Yeah, I had a minute and figured I'd give it another try."

There's a beat of silence and then, "Rux, is every-thing okay?"

I close my eyes and run my hand back over my hair. Of course she'd be able to tell.

"Yeah, I'm fine. It's just—" I start to ask if she's heard anything from Julia about tonight, but I know better. And hell, I don't really want to explain. It will be out in a few hours and she'll see it then. So instead I ask for what I needed earlier. "Sunshine, tell me about your day."

Chapter 15

Rux

*T*he game was fucked.

That news about Baxter getting out beforehand was bullshit. The whole team was off. Out of sync. Late to pass. Missing opportunities we shouldn't have missed. Vassar, who usually plays like a beast, looked like he just woke up. Popov almost scored on us. If it wasn't for Diesel pulling out a last-minute save, we would have been the laughingstock of the league. And me? Hell.

Three trips to the sin bin, zero points. It was rough. Coach looked like he was going to have an aneurysm. And after that dumpster fire of a game, they made the announcement. Baxter came down to the press room from wherever he'd been watching from. Julia stood off to the side. And we watched as he gave an emotional speech about what playing for this team meant to him. About how his life had been about hockey for as long as he could remember. He talked about injuries and overcoming odds and then he talked about the concussions.

He talked about making the hardest choice of his life, and looking forward to finding out what was next.

By the end, Coach looked like he was about to spring a leak, and truth, I got a little choked up myself.

I knew it was coming.

Or at least I'd been telling myself I had. Maybe that wasn't quite true though, because watching Greg shake hands with the GM and take a deep breath before giving the press a final wave—*fuck*.

On the way out, he walked over and pulled me in for a solid hug.

And then he and Julia walked out together, and I felt... deflated.

I didn't call Cammy after, just got my shit together, climbed into my car and headed to her place. I like being alone with Cammy, but most of the time I'm a little bummed I don't get to see Matty after my games. Tonight though, I'm glad the little guy doesn't have to see me when I walk in through her front door and straight into Cammy's arms. She's so much smaller than I am but damn, the girl knows how to hug. She peers up at me and I can see her eyes are a little red.

"That was tough," she says against my chest. "Did you know when I talked to you? Is that what was wrong?"

I take a deep breath of her hair and neck, soaking in that warm vanilla scent of her. "I heard a rumor. Didn't know if it was legit, but I had a feeling."

"Greg didn't talk to you?"

I tell her about the missed call and not being able to connect with him before the game. That I'd known what was coming for months.

"But it's not really the same as having it actually happen," she says, understanding in her eyes.

Reluctantly drawing back, I run a hand over my face. "No, it's not."

My legs feel like lead as she pulls me over to the couch. When we sit, she's too far away, and I manhandle her some, scooping her into my lap to hold her close.

This is what I need.

I lean back and she tucks her head against my shoulder.

"You okay?" The question is soft, gentle like the woman asking it.

"I'm freaking out, Cammy," I admit into the quiet of her apartment. And when her palm flattens against

158

my chest, I cover it with my own. "Don't think I told you, but before I started playing with Greg, I was headed back to the farm team." Hell, I'm not sure they would have even let me play at that point. I take a heavy breath, the past weighing on me like it hasn't for years. "I was losing everything."

She lifts her head, a little stitch pulled between her eyes. "You said you had a sort of rocky start, but I didn't realize it was that… precarious."

"Yeah, not many people did. Hell, at the time I didn't know how close I'd come to losing everything. Found out later, Coach had already made the call to let me go but held off after seeing me with Greg. Decided to see how things played out. What we could do."

Beneath my hand, hers fist in my shirt, holding tight. "I'm glad he did."

"Me too." I lean forward to press a quick kiss to her forehead. "Thing is, it's not like I was playing like crap or something. I was good. *On the ice.* Off the ice I was fucking up. It was a… rough time in my life. I was volatile. Doing stupid shit. Letting my mouth run, looking for trouble. Drinking too much. Fighting." I close my eyes, remembering the torn skin across my knuckles, the blood in my teeth when I saw my reflection in the broken glass over the bar. The bar owner, a friend, telling me to get out. That he didn't want to see my face again. He wasn't the only one. "I'd worked my ass off for so damn long, made so many sacrifices to get where I was, made so many choices that cost me in ways I didn't fully appreciate at the time. All to get my shot, and I was throwing it away."

"God, Rux, why?"

The way she's looking at me, it's like she can't even imagine this other version of me. Like she doesn't believe it. And hell, I've made damn sure I never gave her a reason to suspect that other part of me existed. But tonight, I need her to know. I need her to want me anyway.

"My head wasn't in a good place." I run my hand over her hair, wondering if this time I'll be able to tell her. "I got kind of messed up over this girl."

Her brows lift, but unlike the past times women have come up, there's no teasing lilt to her voice when she echoes, "A girl?"

And I get her surprise. For as long as Cammy has known me, girls have been a passing thing. Casual company. Everyone knows I don't really date in any meaningful way. I'm not looking for forever, I don't want the things most people want.

Marriage.

Kids.

Fuck.

But there was a time it was different.

"We dated in high school and through Juniors." I

can feel the vise tightening on my lungs just thinking about her. Beth. "I thought we'd get married." I'd tried. *I'd begged.*

Cammy is completely still against me. Her eyes wide with shock when she asks, "What happened?"

"I screwed it up." I swallow, hating how insufficient that explanation is. How it doesn't even begin to convey the magnitude of what happened. I want to tell her, but Christ, I can't do it. "Made mistakes. You know me, rash, impulsive. Don't always think before I act. Surprisingly, I wasn't any better at twenty," I say, trying to make light. But Cammy doesn't smile.

"Rux, I had no idea. How do I not know about any of this?"

I clear my throat, take a breath. "Yeah, well, things ended badly. I have... regrets." I remember that damn ring leaving my hand, the light catching on the stone as it catapulted toward the river. That sick feeling twisting my gut, cutting off the air in my lungs. The pain. "Don't really like to talk about it."

I try to say more. Explain. But I can't force the words past the knot strangling my throat. I can't tell her what my actions cost me. How what happened changed me.

Cammy waits, but when I don't say more, that hand over my heart presses closer. "I'm sorry."

Not as much as me. "I was pretty messed up after.

It didn't affect my play right away. But eventually, no one could even see my game past all the bullshit outside of it. I didn't recognize what I was doing, how bad things had gotten. There was just this angry red haze around me all the time, this noise in my head I couldn't tune out."

"I can't even imagine you like that. It breaks my heart to hear about you in so much pain."

I don't deserve her sympathy, but I can't manage to set her straight either. And I can't let Beth spend any more time in my brain than she already has or I'll start thinking about—

Don't go there.

I force another breath, clear my throat, and pull Cammy's hand up for a kiss. "But something happened when Greg and I paired up. Something changed. He recognized the potential before I did, just like he recognized that as good as we were on the ice, what I was doing off the ice could blow it all. I still remember getting into it with one of the guys in the locker room after a practice because I didn't like the way he'd been looking at me or some stupid shit. Greg caught me before I swung and nearly laid me out right there. He got up in my face and didn't get out of it until I could see that this wasn't just about *my shot* in the NHL, that it wasn't just his. That it was our whole team's chance and what we did mattered to a hell of a lot more people than just me or him. That there were mothers and sisters and friends and coaches and mentors behind every one of these guys, all of them making sacrifices… all of them owed the best we could do. By the time he was done, I felt about as low as I could for the way I'd been fucking off. For not getting my head straight and not being a part of the team that needed me."

The corner of her mouth tips up. "So you turned it around."

"I turned it around. Got over myself. Grew a pair. Whatever." My head drops back, and I let out a short breath before meeting her eyes again. "You know the expression 'fake it till you make it'? Man, Greg hammered that shit into my head *hard*. 'Not friendly with the guys on the team? *Fake it.* Ask 'em about their weekend, their mom, their girl. Don't care about the answer? *Fake it.* Get elated about whatever trivial bit of shit they share with you. Get excited about their game. *Just fake it until you don't have to.*'"

Squinting past my shoulder, Cammy shakes her head. "No way. You're so over-the-top friendly and excited about… everything. You're genuine." Her brows pull together. "I know you're not faking it. You can't be."

"Nah. That's the thing, it feels a fuck-ton better being happy than being pissed. It feels *good* to see someone smile, to make them laugh. It's addictive. And yeah, it took a while before I totally meant it, and even longer before my teammates trusted that I wasn't just screwing with them—"

"Because I'm guessing you flipped it on a dime?"

I run my hand over her back, holding her close. "Probably. And they didn't know me before things got dark. The way I am now is a hell of a lot closer to the way I was before things went to shit."

"My man of extremes." There's affection in her words, but I can't help wonder how long it will last before this or one of my other personality "quirks" starts wearing thin. A while, I hope.

"Yeah, yeah. All or nothing. I know. But Baxter was right. It worked. I was seeing more game time, and that haze cleared. The noise in my head went quiet and the cheering crowds got loud. And ever since, we've been a package deal."

"What happens to his career happens to yours," she offers gently. "Same agent. Same teams."

And yeah, she gets it.

"Except his career is over. And I'm not the leader he is. I feel like I'm screwing up again. Falling short. The team is looking to me to step up and deliver something I'm not sure I've got to give without him."

She lets out a soft breath, and peers up at me. "It's going to come together. One way or another. Just give it time." She tucks herself against me again, letting her head rest over my heart and her fingers thread with mine. "I believe in you."

My eyes close at the words that mean more than she could possibly understand.

I should go home soon. Let Cammy get some sleep in her own bed. But I can't make myself let her go yet. I can't give up the comfort of her head against my chest and the silk of her hair beneath my hand.

I hold her until her breath slows and she curls closer. Until it feels like my world isn't being blown apart. And then I hold her some more.

Chapter 16

Cammy

"*B*e good for your dad," I say, giving my little boy a long squeeze.

Jeremy is standing in his doorway, arm propped against the jamb, an affectionate look in his eyes as Matty zips inside.

It's such a change from the first time I brought him over for a solo evening with his dad. Those anxious first steps and tentative looks back having made my son seem years younger than he actually was.

Not anymore.

"You want to come in, hang out a while?" Jeremy asks, triggering that pangy thing my heart does every time I leave Matty. There's always a part of me that wants to stay. That doesn't want to miss out on whatever my boy is getting up to. But it's important for Matty and Jeremy to have time alone, and tonight… well, I'm looking forward to my own plans.

"No, this is your time. You guys have fun."

He looks back, then rubs a hand over his jaw, giving me the same look I used to see back in high school. "We'd have even *more fun* if you stayed."

"Thank you. Really. But I'll see you guys tomorrow." Looking past Jeremy, I call into the apartment. "Bye, Matty. Love you."

He calls back with a quick, "Bye, Mom!" and I'm gone.

Rux has been traveling for the last three days and got in so late last night he went straight home instead of coming over. He spent this morning over at the Children's Hospital hanging out with the kids and then had back-to-back appointments through the rest of the afternoon. Which was for the best, since I had work of my own to finish, and didn't want anything interfering when I finally got to see him tonight.

I drive home with a ridiculous smile on my face, my belly in this constant state of freefall knowing I'm about to see him.

It's been two weeks since Greg announced his retirement and Rux was promoted to team captain, and he's coming around to his new role. Julia thinks the team is still struggling to find their footing with the new lineups, but the Slayers won again last night and I can't wait to celebrate.

By the time I get home, my heart is beating at triple time.

I'm not expecting Rux for another thirty minutes, but my eyes keep darting to the clock, like somehow I have the power to speed it up. There's this fluttery sort of anticipation happening in my belly I haven't felt in so long.

It's crazy. But it feels so good, I can't even try to tell myself to slow down. To hold back.

I'm wearing a thin, soft yellow sweater, rubbing lotion into my legs when I hear the front door, fifteen minutes early.

"Hey, Cammy, you home?"

"Coming!" I fumble the bottle and rush out of my bathroom.

I pause at the hall doorway, my heart doing something crazy when I see him standing there in his dark jeans, an untucked white Oxford straining around his biceps, and his hair combed neatly back from his face.

Rux turns, his eyes raking hot over me, and delivers a growl so sexy, I shudder. And then we're coming together in a crash, his arms catching me as I wrap around him like a koala. My fingers are in his hair, coasting over his heavy jaw, my legs hooked hard against his ass. I'm showering his face with kisses as he carries me to the back of the couch.

He runs his hands over my bare legs where they're wrapped around him and buries his face in my neck. "I missed you."

"Me too," I gasp as he rocks into me just right, making my insides contract with need. "Been watching the clock all day."

Our eyes meet. "Yeah?"

God, I love the look on his face, like he can't quite believe it's true. I swallow past the emotion fast on the rise within me and reach for him again. "Yeah."

We're a frenzy of hands and mouths and bodies in motion. My sweater and his shirt are gone, the scruff of his jaw teases my breasts where they're spilling out of my bra, then teases lower down my belly in a not-so-subtle hint at where he's going, what he wants to do to me.

Hot need grips my core at the thought of Rux and his new favorite pastime.

A needy moan escapes me, but then I'm slipping out of his hold and off the back of the couch to the floor. For as much of an addict as he's made me for his tongue, I've been fantasizing about something else for days.

Going to my knees, I take his jeans and boxers down with me.

"Baby, what are— *Oh fuck.*"

He's leaning over me, the muscles of his powerful arms and chest stand out in stark relief as they brace against the back of the couch, his jeans pushed down to his thick thighs. Overwhelmed, I blink.

This man.

How is this real?

He swallows. "Sunshine, you don't have to," he says, voice thick as he runs a shaky hand over my cheek.

Turning into that devastatingly gentle touch, I rub my face against his palm. "I want to."

So bad.

I run my palms up those hard muscled thighs, up the slabs of his abs and back down the path of that crazy vee until my fingers are teasing soft over his thick length, squeezing lightly and then firmer.

Rux stops breathing as our eyes meet. My lips part and I barely brush them against the hard tip.

"Cammy," he groans, helpless as I take him in my mouth.

I've given blowjobs before, to Jeremy, a million years ago. They were always for *him.* Always an exercise in mechanics. Insert Tab A in Slot B and wait for the warning that it was time to pull away. But this, now? This is a selfish act. One I'm so completely engaged in, I don't think I've ever needed anything as much as I need the silk and steel and taste of Rux on my tongue. So good.

I feel his restraint as I draw him in as far as I can, pull back, and then draw him deeper. There's nothing mechanical about this. It's about emotion and need and this thing between us that's been growing quietly since that ridiculous first kiss.

He gathers my hair, holding it out of my face as I set the pace. My hands slide around the backs of his thighs, and I pull him closer. Then we're rocking together, and he's sliding wet and hard into my mouth as I moan around him.

Gravel-rough praise rains down from above as he meets the back of my throat.

"Baby, you're too... *so good*..."

Each guttural, desperate plea—

"*Losing my mind...*"

—lands between my thighs, making me wetter, hotter, until I slip my fingers into the panties he sent me yesterday. I've never been this turned on. Never been so caught up in needing to give someone else pleasure.

"That's *so hot*..." He's heavy against my tongue, throbbing. His thighs like granite. "Touch yourself, Sunshine... need to see you come... with my cock between your lips... *fuck*!"

That's all it takes and I'm tipping over the edge,

coming hard and then holding him close, swallowing deep as he spills down my throat.

When we both finish, he slides to the floor so we're slumped against the back of the couch. He pulls me into his arms and kisses me long and slow and with such tender affection, something deep in my chest breaks open and I have to blink away the moisture gathering at the corners of my eyes.

"Baby, that was insane," he murmurs, holding me close. Holding me like he'll never let me go. "But this... *this* is what I've been waiting for."

Chapter 17

Rux

"*R*ux!"

       I've got a freshly showered, still-damp Cammy thrown over my shoulder, my hand wrapped around her bare thigh, her laughter tickling my back. The too-long sleeves of my shirt dangle past her fingertips as she grabs my ass and pinches my sides.

"What's that, Sunshine? Can't hear you over the giggling."

It doesn't get any better than this.

"Put me down!"

She's going down on the couch where she rocked my world a few hours back, and then I'm going down on her. But first the kitchen.

She grabs the doorway as I carry her past. And

yeah, I'm getting off in no small way from the play fight she's putting up. It makes me wonder how much fun we could have at my place. Way more room for a game of chase.

"You need a glass of water or something?" After what we did in her bedroom, maybe a Gatorade. And after the shower, hell, maybe two. "I'm gonna grab that whipped cream."

She freezes, that squirming, wriggling body going stone still.

"Cammy?" I'd have sworn she'd be into the whipped cream.

"*Oh shit*, Rux, put me—"

"Mommy? What are you doing up there?"

My head snaps around to where Matty's standing behind us, a pinched look on his sort of green face. In the next second, Jeremy's there behind him, eyes wide with horror as he looks from Matty to us and back.

Fuck me.

———

Cammy

THERE ISN'T anything dignified about my dismount from Rux's shoulder, especially considering my ass isn't covered by anything but a pair of panties that say "That's my pie" in script across the front.

"Matty, baby, what are you doing here?" I croak, but it only takes a second to see and then feel as he rushes over to me, burying his warm little forehead into my stomach. Thank God this shirt goes almost to my knees. "Honey, are you sick?"

He nods pitifully. I stroke his sweat-damp hair and, holding him closer, turn to Jeremy who's standing awkwardly at the kitchen doorway.

"Shi—oot. Cammy, I'm sorry. He seemed fine earlier. We had dinner and played a game. He wasn't complaining or anything, but then about forty minutes ago, he groaned once and puked."

Matty looks past me to Rux who's standing stone still in his boxer briefs and nothing else. Oh my God. My poor baby. What's he thinking walking in on this?

"Rux, I vomited in his ficus."

"That's sounds rough, little man. I'm sorry you're not feeling good."

Matty nods. "Why are you wearing your underwear?"

I'm going to die.

Rux opens his mouth and then closes it again, shooting me a helpless look.

"I spilled our dinner," I say too quickly, feeling the

flames of Hell licking at my feet for flat-out lying to my boy. "It got everywhere."

"Everywhere," Rux echoes.

Matty nods, too wiped to press for details. "Everyone makes mistakes."

Jeremy clears his throat and starts to step into the kitchen, stops short and then sort of waves for Matty to come to him. "Hey, kiddo, how about we go put your stuff in your room and get you into some PJs for Mom."

I have never been more grateful to anyone than I am in that moment.

I watch my son take his father's hand, feeling like I can't breathe. Like I'm never going to be able to come back from this. Like it's all fun and games until your seven-year-old son walks in on you wearing a man's shirt with your ass in the air.

"Cammy, come on." Rux takes my hand. "Let him put his stuff away and we'll get changed."

I nod as he leads me back to the bedroom… where I stop and stare, guilt cramping my stomach. It looks like the clothes exploded off our bodies in here.

"*Sunshine.*"

"It's okay." Frantic, I start grabbing stray socks and jeans and belts and shoes, shoving all of it into his hands. "Hurry."

I pull on the leggings I never got to before Rux

arrived. Socks. An elastic for my hair. "I'm going to go check on Matty. What do we do? You can't slip out."

"No, I'll say goodbye to him and then take off." He's standing there in his jeans, bare chested. The way he's built, it's hard to imagine him ever being anything but confident and sure. But the way he's rubbing the back of his neck, his mouth sort of caught between a smile and frown, says that's not how he feels. "I mean. If you want me to. I could stay and help. I'd like to."

"Maybe not tonight. He's sick. And you don't want to catch anything, right? Rux, where's your shirt? We need to go."

He lets out a gruff laugh. "Babe. *You're wearing it.*"

I look down. *Shit.*

Another flash change, and I'm ready. Jeremy is waiting for me outside Matty's door, not quite meeting my eyes.

"I'm really sorry, Cammy. I tried to call but there wasn't any answer and it went from fine to meltdown crying about wanting to go home in a blink. He said you'd be home, and he had a key and… Shit, he was so upset and wanted to be home and—I didn't think."

"No, Jeremy. I'm sorry." He'd been trying to call, and the reason I didn't hear it was because I'd been in the shower with Rux. My son needed me, and I wasn't there.

I feel sick.

"I always have my phone, and this time—"

He holds up a hand, shaking his head, a half-pained, half-pleading look in his eyes. "I get it."

The awkward apologies go back and forth for another minute, and then Matty steps out of his room, the stuffed animal he decided to leave behind this morning clutched against his chest.

"Where's Rux?" he asks, and I catch the slightest wince from Jeremy.

"Right here, my man." Rux ducks out of my room, completely dressed.

"You're leaving? But I just got here," Matty whines, looking completely pathetic.

Rux's eyes cut to mine. He offered to stay. But... I look away.

"Sorry," he says easily. "I need to take off. But I'll check in to see how you're doing tomorrow."

They bust knuckles and Rux gives me a quick kiss on the top of my head.

I turn to Jeremy. "You don't need to stay. I've got this. Go clean up your ficus and see if it's salvageable."

Rux hangs back, waiting. But Jeremy runs a hand over his mouth. "So, I was wondering..." He clears his throat and shoots a quick glance at Rux before turning back to me. Voice low, he leans closer. "Cammy, I know it's my own fault that I have no idea how to take care of our son when he's sick. But I want that to change. I want a lot of things to change. Do you think maybe I *could* stay? So the next time he's at my place, if something like this happens, I don't have to bring him home."

What he's saying makes perfect sense, but the part of me that's not entirely rational... That's possessive of the son I've raised alone bristles at the idea of Matty being anywhere but with me when he's sick.

Selfishly, I want to be the only one who can give him the comfort he needs.

But that's exactly what it is... Selfish.

My eyes cut to Rux where he's still waiting for me to boot Jeremy out like I have him.

I've already been too selfish tonight.

What if I hadn't been here? What if I'd been out on the lake for one of those summer booze cruises Rux invited me to last summer? What if I couldn't get back?

More than being the one Matty turns to when he feels bad, I want my son to have the security of knowing, even if I'm not around, there are other people who can take care of him, who love him.

So as sour as the words taste on my tongue, I say them anyway.

"Sure. Of course, you can stay."

Chapter 18

Rux

"*Oomph!*"

I sail across the ice on my back, muttered f-bombs dropping in my wake.

That's what I get for having my head up my ass instead of on the drills, the puck, and the players who got screwed having to practice with me this morning.

I'm off my game after last night. Cammy was so upset. Matty walking in on us freaked her out. Hell, of course it did. She doesn't want him building up expectations about something that isn't going to happen. We've been so careful about how we act in front of him, and in one moment all those efforts went to crap. I get it.

But watching her close down, shut me out—fuck, that was brutal. And then that bullshit with Jeremy standing there, looking like all he cared about was learning how to take care of his son, pissed me off. I'm sure he cares about Matty. It's impossible not to. But I've seen the way he looks at Cammy, the way he looks at me. And last night was *a move*.

One I need to put aside.

"Aww shit, sorry, man," Kellog says, cutting to a sharp stop beside me, a guilty look in his eyes. "Thought you were—" He shakes his head. "You okay? Didn't ring your bell, did I?"

"No, man." Thank fuck. I'd never forgive myself for letting the team down if I'd cost them another player with a concussion. "Don't sweat it. Totally my fault. I'm fine."

Circling back into position, he points his stick at me. "Sure?"

"I'm sure." I won't let it happen again.

We run a few more drills and I get my head together, find that place where there's only the game. By the time the whistle blows, I'm pouring off sweat and feeling more like a player and less like a jealous boyfriend. But it's still there, hovering at the edge of my mind.

Are we good?

How late did Jeremy stay?

Did he try something?

Did he make her smile? Jesus.

I'll feel better when I talk to my girl. I want to hear her voice. I want to see her eyes. And hell, maybe I want to hear her tell me what a tool Jeremy is. How useless. How Matty didn't care if he was there or not.

Only as soon as I think that, I feel like the world's biggest shithead because who wishes that on anyone? What I ought to be hoping for is Jeremy stepping up as the best damn dad the world's ever seen. Because I want it for Matty.

I do.

But I want something else for Cammy. Something better than the selfish prick who abandoned her when she needed him most. If I thought that I was good enough, I'd have put a ring on her finger already. But I want more for her. I want the best. But first, I want just a little more time with her before she finds it.

I hit the showers and get cleaned up. Have lunch with the guys.

We've got a game tonight, but I've got an hour or so to kill.

"Hey, Sunshine, how's the sickie?" I ask from the car, hoping maybe I'll be able to stop over.

"How does one little body produce that much puke?"

"That bad, huh?" There's a weary groan through the line and I hate the sound of it. "How about I come over and give you a hand for a while? Bring you something to eat."

There's no missing the hesitation before she answers. "Matty just fell asleep and I think I'm going to try and grab some myself while I can. Raincheck?"

"Yeah, for sure. Get some rest and tell Matty to feel better."

I mean it. She needs a break.

But there's a part of me that keeps seeing the way she looked at me—or more like didn't look at me—when she turned down my offer to stay. And that part can't help wondering if she would have said yes if last night hadn't happened.

Cammy

"*FOUR DAYS!* But you've talked to him, right?" Julia demands through the line. She's in LA again and watching the game with me over the phone. "You didn't just kick him out and then go radio silent. Right?"

I roll my eyes, taking it on faith she can sense it. "Yes, I talked to him. Mostly texting though. I was exhausted from staying up with Matty puking for two days." That much is true. "Our schedules were off and then he had to leave." Technically, also true. Though I could have made it work. A week ago, I would have. I'd have been waiting by the door for him to show up after the game, my heart racing, my body aching for the chance to get close to him. To feel his arms around me, his heart beating against mine.

"Okay. Besides, this is Rux. More than two missed calls and he would have the whole team involved. WAGs posting flyers, the fire department breaking down your door and some tactical team swinging in through your windows."

I try to laugh, but Julia must hear something off with it because suddenly her voice is serious, quiet. "Hey, Cammy, what's going on? Everything okay with you guys?"

My mouth opens to tell her yes, but the words won't come. I take a breath. "I want it to be. But Julia... *what am I doing?*"

God, I wish she was here right now. I love what she's doing with her career, and I love that she and Greg are setting the bar for relationship goals. But the little sister in me misses the nights when we'd sit and talk until we were too tired to talk anymore. I miss the comfort of her arm around me when I'm anxious and knowing that before she was anyone else's she was mine.

It's selfish. But I miss her.

"I don't understand. What do you mean?" she asks. "I thought things were good with you guys. Fun and sexy and... all the good stuff."

"It is. It's amazing." I shake my head, suddenly overwhelmed by emotion I can't account for. "He makes me feel like I'm alive in a way I haven't been in seven years." Maybe ever. "Like all the things I started wondering if I would ever find... are suddenly within reach."

"But that's good, right?"

"I'm not sure it is. I mean, it feels good." So good. "But Matty was never supposed see us together like that. What if he starts getting his hopes up about Rux and I getting serious when it can't happen?"

Julia *hmm*s through the line. "Okay, first, it's time to face facts. You're already serious. No matter what your official relationship status is, you and Rux have been serious from way before you started whatever it is you started."

"But—"

"Second, the only thing that's going to hurt Matty *if* things don't work out, is *if* he loses Rux. I mean, so what if the kiddo catches you and Rux K.I.S.S.I.N.G.? It's not like it was with Mom cycling through her losers, going from zero to moved-in-with-us in the course of one night."

"Handing over our lunch money so he could grab some smokes the next day." I close my eyes, hating those memories. The confusion and fear when the next guy showed up. Wondering how long he'd last, and whether I'd wish it had been shorter by the end.

Restless, I walk over to the windows and look down to the snow-covered streets. Matty's going to need boots tomorrow. "I know it's different with Rux." Aside from Julia, he's as close to a constant as we've had in our lives.

"Good. Because that brings me to my third point... I'm not sure it's just Matty you're trying to protect. I think you're falling for Rux. I think this thing between you has gotten more real than either of you expected, and now that you've stopped to think, you're terrified of what that means."

I close my eyes and rest my head against the cool glass.

Of course, she'd see what I've been trying not to.

"I know better. Julia, I don't want to keep making the same mistakes. Rux isn't looking for forever. He's made it clear from the start he isn't interested in being anyone's happily ever after." I know this. I understand it. *I agreed to it.*

"But you said you weren't interested in anything

more either. Isn't it possible he might have changed his mind too? Believe me, he wouldn't be the first commitment-phobe to convert for the right girl."

The right girl.

What if I could be the one? What if my happily ever after has been right in front of me all this time? What if Rux has already fallen in love with our family?

I blink, my breath catching almost painfully on the what-ifs I never let myself consider.

"Did—did he say something to Greg?"

"Not that I know of. But then the comparing notes kind of stopped once you guys started looking less like an itch needing a scratch and more like the start of something that might go the distance." After a weighted beat, she asks, "Do you want me to ask?"

"No, no. Don't. I just need to stop freaking out and talk to him."

"Soon, Cammy."

"Soon."

"Good. Do you need water or a snack?" she asks, almost like she's right beside me. Like she's been looking out for me since we were kids. "There's only a minute left before third period starts."

"Let me pee real quick and I'll be right back."

The guys end up with a win and I talk to Rux for a few minutes on the plane before they take off, but it's a quick call and, honestly, I can't tell if that thin layer of underlying tension is coming from him or me. I toss and turn through most of the night, hating that I haven't seen him since Friday night as much as I hate the questions running through my mind on repeat since talking to Julia.

Not whether I was falling for Rux. The second she said it, I knew it was true.

But what it means for us if nothing has changed for Rux. What kind of strain it would put on our friendship if he realizes how I feel. Whether letting my heart get away from me has cost me a friendship so critical I can't even imagine my life without it. What it means for Matty.

My office is in Julia's old bedroom, and I've been logged in to the hospital, working through charts, correcting and filling in coding since five. I took a break to get Matty off to school and then worked through lunch. But my mind keeps slipping back to the what-ifs I don't want to think about but can't ignore just the same. I'm going crazy.

"Hey, Sunshine."

I drop my headset and jerk to my feet, half of me wanting to fling myself into his arms, the other half convinced I need to hold back. "I didn't hear you come in."

He's got his shoulder propped at the doorway and from the still damp, combed-back hair, worn jeans and muscle-hugging thermal, I'm guessing he came straight over after waking up. He looks so good my heart actually aches seeing him.

The corner of his mouth slants and he looks at me with eyes that tell me he knows something's up.

Would it even be possible to go back to being just friends from this? Is there still a chance?

"*Cammy,*" he says, like some part of him is aching too and suddenly my feet are moving and all those what-ifs I've been clinging to don't exist.

My arms close around his neck, and the tension and anxiety lifts from my shoulders as he groans into my hair and then lifts me from the floor. "Christ, I missed you."

Toes dangling above the hardwood, I tip my head back. "I missed you too."

That half smile pulls into the real thing and he kisses me, walking us into the living room and around to the couch. When he tucks me into his lap, I snuggle in.

His arms tighten around me in the most heavenly way, and for a minute we just breathe, my head on his shoulder, his big hand smoothing down my spine.

"About the other night," Rux starts, a hesitancy in his voice I don't normally associate with this man.

"Yeah, about that." I swallow. "Not exactly the way you imagined our evening going, I'm guessing."

"No, it wasn't. But there's no other place I'd want him to be when he's sick than with you. Sure, it would've been nice to be wearing pants when the poor kid came in, but… hell, Cammy, I just wish you'd have let me stay and help you."

He doesn't mention Jeremy, but I know it bothered him.

"I'm sorry. I freaked out. For seven years, I've never dropped my son off without it being front and center in my mind that I might be needed to pick him back up. That whatever event I'm attending, no matter how much it might mean to me, or how much fun I'm having, I am *available* if that boy needs me. He's first in my mind every single time. No exceptions."

"Only this time you didn't check your phone," he says, gruffly. "Because you were with me."

Emotion tightens my chest, makes me blink back tears.

"He was sick and he needed me. And he was so sure that I would be there for him, he convinced his dad to bring him back here without talking to me. And then what does he walk in on, but—"

"His mom having some fun." At my look he winces. "It wasn't ideal. But it could have been a lot worse."

My cheeks flame thinking about the dirty promises Rux had been making that night. What might have been going on if Matty had shown up ten minutes later.

"Hey, come on, don't hide."

Slowly, I lift my head from where it's buried against his chest. "Nothing like that has ever happened with him. I've never brought a man back here. I've never let him down."

He catches my chin. "You didn't let him down. You dropped everything the second you knew he needed you. And even if Matty had to wait, it wasn't long, and he was with his *father*."

I nod, but that guilt is still chewing at me. And not just that.

I pinch my lips together.

I need to know where we stand. If maybe it's on the same page... Only, I've spent too much time imagining Rux's reaction if I ask him flat-out and his feelings haven't changed.

"I got worried about what he might think, seeing us that way. I mean, I know this isn't forever. That we're... just having some fun and all." It's a copout, but I can't risk damaging our friendship. So I pause, waiting to see if maybe he'll disagree. If he'll show me that wildly passionate side and flip me over so he's on top, press kisses against my mouth around telling me how he's decided he'll never give me up.

But instead of telling me this is the thing he never

expected either, the happily ever after he didn't think he wanted but now can't live without, he takes my hand in his and pulls it up to his mouth for a quick kiss. "The best kind of fun, Sunshine. But I get it, and we'll be careful around Matty. I don't want him to be disappointed or confused when we put the *just* back in our friendship either."

That place I never expected Ruxton Meyers to touch starts to crumble. He doesn't want more. He doesn't want less either, which is the only reason I hold it together.

Ducking my head, I breathe through the raw pain in my chest.

I thought I'd braced for it. I thought I'd talked myself out of hoping. But apparently, not so much.

This isn't the start of our forever after all.

It's okay. It's good I know. Yes, it hurts. But I've had to accept worse.

And I'll accept this.

I knew what Rux's limits were going in, and no matter how good this feels, they haven't changed. I can live with that, and even when this thing between us has run its course—our friendship will still be enough. More.

"Hey, Cammy." The eyes that meet mine are completely devoid of the humor and joking that always live within. "I will never let that little boy down.

I'd crawl over hot coals for him. You know I'll always be there for the both of you, right?"

I nod, my eyes filling with tears. "I do. It's one of the reasons I love you so much."

"Funny, it's one of the reasons I love you too."

Chapter 19

Rux

$\mathcal{I}$ hang with Cammy as long as I can, using the living room to catch up on some calls while she works in her office. I feel about a million times better now that I've gotten to hold her and talk to her, find out where her head was at with everything after the other night. Yeah, there was that minute when I thought she might be trying to feel me out about taking things to a more serious level. But I'm chalking it up to not enough sleep on my end. Because then she'd seemed fine, and seriously, Cammy knows better than to get any ideas about me.

And I sure as hell know better than to let myself get ideas about her.

Matty blows in like a whirlwind after school, all

hugs and math sheets and news about the play coming up. Which I'm fucking bummed falls on a game night, so there's no chance I can make it. Matty understands, but it still sucks.

There's a late practice, so I haul out with another round of hugs and Cammy giving me that sunshine smile that makes me wish I didn't have to go, but I'm already pushing it enough that by the time I make it to the rink, I've got to run from the parking lot to make practice on time.

"Yo, Rux," Assistant Coach Mateo calls out, waving me over. "GM wants to see you in his office."

I stop in my tracks, mentally rolling back through the last few days for anything obvious that would have me called in to the principal's office. I did walk through the hotel lobby on my hands—but I'm *good* at it. I stayed away from all the guests. I had all my clothes on. Wait, did I? Yeah, I did.

Shit, shit, shit.

If I didn't do anything seriously stupid, then there's only one reason I can think for why I'd be getting called up there.

A trade.

Cammy's eyes flash through my mind. Matty's grin.

Christ, I don't want to give them up. I don't—

"He say why?" They never say why.

"Just to send you up when you got here."

I drop my bag at the security desk and then take the stairs two at a time to the second floor where the offices are located, scrolling through the hockey feeds as I go. No news of a Slayers trade. My agent didn't know anything when I talked to him earlier.

I take a breath, every loss, blown shot, and missed opportunity rolling through my mind on fast forward. I stretch my neck and repeat three times, "I'm not getting traded."

The General Manager's door opens before I knock, and Coach Adkins meets my eyes with a glare. "About time. Jesus, Meyers, get in here."

The office is packed with three coaches and a guy who looks about as comfortable as I feel.

From behind his desk, Marty Sheely waves a meaty hand between us. "Danny Whalen, meet your new captain, Ruxton Meyers. Rux, Danny's our new center, coming up from the farm team. Why don't you show him around."

I start to breathe again. Give the universe a mental high five and, after shaking a few hands and promising the GM I'll get the kid situated, get out of there.

Ten minutes later, we're down in the locker room where I'm getting Danny and the team up to speed.

"Okay, so Popov and O'Brian both sport chubs in here—"

"Jesus, one fucking time," O'Brian bitches.

"So if you feel something graze your thigh... my money's on them. Vsev is not the guy to go to for advice on birth control. You want to stay out of jail, probably better keep your distance from Bowie, Static, and Diesel. Got a picture of your mom on your phone?"

Danny nods, his mouth caught between a smile and frown. "Yeah?"

"Don't show it to Bear. Tucker's prickly. If Grady here looks like he's feeling you out, don't get excited. His brother's getting married this summer and it's looking like there's no line he won't cross to make sure he's got a date when he goes home."

"Come on, man," Grady sighs, shaking his head. "Loan me Cammy for the weekend and I'll leave the rookie alone."

Dude. Did *not*.

Grady's hands come up as he backs away. "Whoa, kidding, Rux. *Kidding.*"

Better be.

Vassar flashes that thing he calls a smile. "So in case you missed it, don't joke about Cammy."

"Words to live by," O'Brian chimes in.

I shake out my fist. See whose next. "And Kellog... Kellog's good people. We should hang out more."

A whistle blows and I look around. "Time's up.

You'll have to meet the rest of the team on your own. Team, here's what you need to know about Whalen, he's fast as fuck, hungry as hell, spent two years with the farm team, grew up in Virginia, likes oatmeal but not oatmeal cookies, favorite song is 'Believe' by Cher, and has a pet snake he isn't allowed to keep at the hotel and needs a volunteer to house and feed it until he finds a place of his own."

I slap the kid on the back and head over to my stall to suit up for practice. My phone pings and thinking it might be Cammy, I check. It's from the Slayers PR guy. And he wants to know what the hell is up with me and Greg's reporter/stalker Stuart Waters.

Ah shit.

———

Cammy

"I DON'T GET IT. He's suggesting that I've got something to do with how the team is performing this season." I fill my glass from the tap and slide back into my chair at the kitchen table. "That doesn't make any sense."

Rux is sitting beside me, his body language casual, but there's a tension in his eyes I can't miss. He's bothered more than he wants me to know. Enough that he came here straight from practice and hasn't stuck his head in the fridge yet.

"No, it doesn't. And I don't think it's anything we need to worry about. But I wanted to make sure you knew what was going on, since he mentioned you."

My hands come up in confusion, because I just don't get why. Rux shakes his head.

"Waters has got a thing about Greg. He doesn't think he would have retired if it weren't for Julia. He's been pretty vocal about his lack of confidence when it comes to me taking over as captain, and now he's gone and blown any shred of credibility he might have had by suggesting that my being with you—Julia's sister—is cursing the team. It's bullshit. But there are always a few nut jobs out there." He rubs a hand over his face. "I'm sorry you have to deal with any of them."

"Don't be sorry." I lean closer and cover his hand with mine. Smile when he flips his and threads our fingers together. "I don't love being the downfall of the Slayers Hockey organization," I tease. "But I've been around this stuff since the first time Julia went live." Granted, I'm not usually called out by name. But there's been stuff before.

"Look, I know the security in your building is good, but—"

"It's very good." It's why Julia picked this place. "Hey, it sounds like this guy is just spouting off. I mean, there isn't any reason to think it'll go further, right?"

If there was, Rux would have led with it.

"No." He takes a breath and rubs a hand down his face. "I just don't like you ending up in the spotlight because of me."

My phone starts to vibrate across the table, Jeremy's name flashing across the screen.

"Go ahead and get that. It might be about Matty." He gives my hand a squeeze but doesn't let go and for some reason it makes my heart beat a little harder for him.

"Hi Jeremy, what's up?" I ask, eyes still locked with Rux's.

"Cammy, have you seen this article?" he barks through the line, voice tight and loud. "Some asshole called you out as the reason Ruxton Meyers can't get his shit together on the ice."

I close my eyes as heat splashes through my cheeks. When I open them, Rux is still watching, his mouth twisted into a smirk that says he's heard it and everything else someone could say about his game before. I try to pull my hand free of his, hoping to block the sound, maybe go to the other room. But Rux holds on.

"I know about it."

"Babe, are you okay?"

Rux raises a brow, the slant of his smile increasing even as his eyes harden. He mouths, *Babe?*

Something tells me I'll never hear that out of Rux's mouth again.

"This reporter never should have had your name. Meyers should know how to protect you."

"Jeremy—"

"Look, don't freak out. I'm coming over."

This time I manage to free my hand from Rux's and push up from my seat. "Jeremy, stop. Thank you, but we're fine. Rux is here and honestly, I'm not concerned."

There's a pause and I can feel Rux waiting to see how he fills it.

"Is he… staying?"

I blink.

Balls, Rux mouths, and I take a breath, trying not to bristle at the question that's none of Jeremy's business.

"He's not. It's one article. There's no reason to. But if anything changes, I promise to keep you in the loop."

Rux

WATERS DOESN'T QUIT, but at least he leaves Cammy out of his smear campaign. The guy has it out for me, and while I normally wouldn't give two shits about what someone like him is posting, there've been rumblings about changes in the Slayers organization beyond pulling Danny Whalen up, and everyone's feeling more vulnerable than normal.

I tell the guys it's bullshit. That the best way we can protect what we have is not to let rumors get in our heads and to focus on our play. We all know it's true, but when we fall apart in the next two games, it's clear I failed to drive it home the way they deserve.

Getting off the plane, the guys are quiet, heading to the cars without the usual trash talk and joking around. We'll bounce back tomorrow. Tonight, all I want is to see Cammy. I want to get lost in her kiss and her smile and the smell of her hair when I hold her close and bury my face in it. I want that feeling of peace and contentment I only ever really find around her. The calm that doesn't come easy to me.

Once I dump my gear in the trunk, I climb into the driver's seat and pull out my phone to text that I'm on my way. There's a voicemail from an unknown number. My agent mentioned I'd be getting a call from one of the companies we closed an endorsement deal with last week, so I click through to listen. I'm expecting some overly enthusiastic voice to boom through the line looking to coordinate meetings. I'm not expecting the hesitant voice of the ghost from my past.

Beth.

My gut turns to lead and my skin feels itchy and tight as she stammers about getting my number from my mother. How she's sorry for calling after all this time but a reporter contacted her. That he was asking questions. She didn't tell him anything, but she thought I should know.

I disconnect the phone and climb out of the car. I need to breathe. I need to move. I need to put my fist into the concrete pylon in the garage, but somehow there's enough going on upstairs I don't do it.

She didn't tell him anything.

It won't be a story.

No one is going to know.

Cammy and Matty won't—

I walk a few feet, stop in front of the garbage bin, and vomit.

Chapter 20

Rux

ucking Jeremy.

This guy is on my list. And yeah, the last couple weeks haven't been the most chill of my career, but I'm handling it. And I'm standing firm in my assertion... *it's him*, not me, who's the asshole.

I get that he wants to spend time with Matty. But lately, the guy seems to be finding one reason after another to be around. Particularly when I've got a game night or I'm out of town.

Case in point, the chode is parked on Cammy's couch, looking for all the world like he's settled in for a night at home with his family.

Babe, I'm already at the store. Just tell me what you need and let me save you a trip.

What a guy.

And with the *babe* business again. Every time he "slips up" it's followed by that sorry, not sorry shrug and some bullshit about old habits dying hard. I'm never calling her babe again.

Fuck. Him.

I should have pushed harder when I offered that grocery service six months ago. Because now Matty's gone and invited *Special Delivery Dad* to dinner and Cammy, being the softy she is, said yes.

My teeth are about to turn to dust with the way I'm grinding them.

It's the perfect night to be up against the Epics. I need an outlet. That said, I really don't want to leave, but O'Brian's downstairs waiting for me.

"Time to go?" Cammy asks, looking up from the meal I won't be able to stay for, but Jeremy will. Matty vaults over the back of the couch, apologizing to his mom even as he skids up to me.

He grins. "I've been practicing jumping the boards so I can be like you."

And hell, my heart melts right there, my mind blinking back to that night right before Jeremy moved back. It had been him and me while Cammy was out with the girls. He'd looked up at me with those solemn little eyes and told me he wished I could be his dad.

I'd had to take a couple of breaths before I could

answer. Before I could tell him the truth, that I would have been the luckiest guy in the world if I'd gotten to be his dad. But that I was happy I got the next best thing—which was being his friend.

He'd wrapped his arms around me while my heart fucking broke.

There are not words for how much I love this kid.

Cammy laughs, ruffling his hair, and I go down on my knee and give him a hug.

"Nice technique, little man."

I cut a glance out to the living room where Jeremy is studying his phone. Shit. Now, I kind of feel for the guy. Can't be easy hearing your kid say that to another man. But he wouldn't have to if he'd realized how damn lucky he was from the start. If he'd stayed instead of throwing away what another man would have been done anything to hold on to.

"Good luck, Rux. I'm going to watch part of the game tonight and the rest tomorrow after school."

"Awesome. Knowing I've got you cheering for me from home always makes me play better."

Matty skates off and, for a minute, it's just Cammy and me in the kitchen. Her hand at my chest, soft blue eyes peering up at me. Damn.

"Have a good game." Pushing to her toes, she presses a quick kiss to my jaw. My hand at her hip tightens. I want to kiss her so bad right now, but her eyes flare in warning and then she's backing away with a smile that says no dice.

"Call me after the game?" she asks quietly.

"Always." The way our eyes hold makes it both easier and harder to walk out the door.

Jeremy gets up, presumably to move in on my spot beside Cammy while she cooks. *Dick.*

Except instead of pulling out another *babe* and standing too close to the girl he gave up any right to seven years ago… he heads toward me.

"Gotta grab something from the car, I'll walk out with you." There's a clank from the kitchen and then Cammy's in the doorway, her brows pulled together. He smiles at her. "Back in a minute, Cam."

What the hell is this?

We walk out together, exchanging strained smiles as we head to the elevator.

He's up to something and I have a pretty good idea what it is.

He waits until we're inside and turns to me. "I want them back."

It takes a second for the no-bullshit statement to land but when it does, I shake my head at the balls this asshole has saying that to me, especially within a confined space like this. He can't even run. "*What?*"

"I know you're together and you can take my head off without batting an eye. But this is Cammy and my son. This is the family we should have been." He runs a hand over his face and meets my eyes. "I have to try."

"*This time.* That's what you're saying, right? You have to try to man up to your responsibilities and commitments to Cammy and Matty *this time.* The way you didn't the first time or at all through the last seven years. And since we're clarifying, you want Cammy back, but Matty you never had. Because you were gone before he was born? Left a note or something, right?"

This guy is the worst kind of—

"I was a coward. *A kid.* And you're right. I missed years with my son that I'll never get back. I'm ashamed of what I did. It was the worst mistake of my life, but I'm ready to make it right."

My fists clench with my teeth.

"A mistake?" I snap, ignoring the pained honesty in his eyes. Hating it. Hating him. "It was *her life*, Jeremy. You had your chance to be a part of it. And you pissed it away."

And yeah, that burns so bad. Why does *he* get to come back from the worst mistake of his life? From his shame. Why does the guy who *threw away* everything that mattered get the second chance?

"Rux, man, I've spent years working to get to a point where I had something to offer them."

The elevator doors open and we step out, pent-up hostility and aggression pouring out with us. "So the wife in Germany was just some practical, hands-on experience too? I'm sure Cammy really appreciates that. Hell, she probably would have liked to return the favor, but turns out she was too busy raising your kid *alone* to score the practice husband."

He gulps, looking away. "I'm going to make it up to them."

"Oh okay." I give the guy an incredulous look. "What the fuck? You say that and I'm supposed to just shake your hand and step aside. Kiss Cammy on the cheek, pat Matty's head... *and leave*? Not happening, man."

"You ready to put a ring on her finger?"

The question hits me like a sucker punch, knocking the air from my lungs. And just like that, Jeremy has the upper hand. And he knows it.

A nod. "What I thought. Well, I am. If Cammy ever gives me another chance, that's it. I'm all in and I'll never let her down again. I can make her happy, make us the family we should have been. She wants security. I can give it to her. Can you?"

"Are you kidding me?"

He stares me down. "I heard there are rumors of a trade."

I swallow. Fight the urge to check my phone.

"That's all they are. Rumors." For now. At least they were the last time I checked. But with Baxter out for good, everyone's been watching. Waiting to see how all the pieces fall into place. Which ones don't. "If it happened, they could come with me."

Jesus. I can't believe I said that. But the words were out before I could tell myself I wasn't allowed to. That I'm not supposed to want that.

Jeremy snorts at the ceiling. "Tear her away from everyone she loves so you can spend half your season leaving her alone in a city where she knows no one, where the support structure she's built for herself over all these years is nonexistent. And what if the next city isn't a fit? What if you end up traded again the next year... just as soon as Cammy and Matty start to lay down roots?"

Next year, or hell, the next month. There are guys who've been traded nine times in one season. And while that's extreme, there's no guarantee I won't be moving again the next month or a few after that.

In some ways my career is as unpredictable as I am.

It's never bothered me before. Or maybe, it's more that I've never had a reason that it would.

"And I know I'm not on your radar with all this, but if you uproot Matty from his school and friends, you'll also be taking him from the only grandparents he's ever known and the father he's just getting back. Because how the hell am I supposed to leave the job I've had for less than a year, pick up and move, find a new job when there's every chance you might end up moving again a few months later? How is Matty going to feel about having to give me up?"

"We don't know that any of that is going to happen," I say, my throat sounding like it's coated with sandpaper.

Jeremy looks at me hard. "You really selfish enough to think that Cammy would be happy like that? That a life like that would be good for Matty—hell, for anyone except you?" He shakes his head and turns back to go upstairs again. "Think about it, man. I know you care about them. Maybe it's time you show it."

Cammy

WHEN JEREMY COMES BACK EMPTY-HANDED, I lower my voice and ask, "You going to tell me what that was about?"

He gives me a warm smile and a wink. "Later."

I check my phone, but nothing from Rux.

Me: Everything okay?

Rux: That guy wants you.

A part of me wants to tell him he's off base, but all it takes is looking up and finding Jeremy watching me from over our son's head, seeing the look he isn't even trying to hide in his eyes, and I can't.

And that isn't something I've been expecting, though everyone else seemed to be.

Years ago this would have been a dream come true for me. Literally. I couldn't even begin to count how many times I woke up with tears in my eyes having imagined Jeremy coming back. Wanting me back. Wanting us.

But now... there's no elation. No joy. Just the gnawing anxiety that this man isn't someone I can count on. And if he's not actually here for Matty, or if he is, but only because he's thinking package deal... then what does it mean for my son when I tell his father no? Will Jeremy disappear from his life as quickly as he returned?

I feel sick at the thought of my baby having to go through that kind of rejection. That kind of heartache.

I need to talk to Jeremy tonight.

Dinner happens in a rush, and I let Matty and Jeremy handle the bulk of the conversation then ask Matty to take a shower instead of a bath, so I have few minutes alone with his dad.

"Rux seems to think you might be interested in me

again," I say from the kitchen doorway so I can make sure Matty is gone.

Jeremy watches me for a moment, and then leans back in the chair Rux usually takes. "He's right."

"Is that why you're here? Is that why you're back? Because if you've been going to all this trouble with Matty, making him believe that he's the—"

"Whoa, no, Cammy." He shakes his head, shoving out of his seat to walk toward me. And then his hand is on my arm and his face is in front of mine, eyes searching and intense. "I would never use our son for anything. Yes, I want you. I want both of you."

I blow out an unsteady breath, relief relaxing the muscles that had gone tight.

"But what if you can't have me?"

Jeremy straightens, takes a step back, and then leans against the fridge.

"Then it means Matty will have two totally committed parents who love him with their whole hearts… just separately. But Cammy, I need you to believe me. I wouldn't have come back, I wouldn't have gone to the lengths I did with work and finding a place, changing my whole life, if I wasn't committed to being a part of his. I'm not gonna lie, I want you. Since we've been apart, there's been something missing—"

"Jeremy, you married another woman. You lived as

husband and wife in another country for two years. And when you came back, it wasn't to me. So, if you don't mind saving the something-missing routine, I'd appreciate it."

I look back around the corner, the shower still running, no sign of my little guy.

"Why do you think it didn't work out? Because *she knew there was someone else*," he argues. "We both did. I never stopped loving you."

My throat is tight, and I can feel tears at the backs of my eyes. I don't want to cry in front of this man. I don't want to shed another tear because of him, not ever for the rest of my life.

"Cammy." He reaches for me, but I bat his hand away.

"Don't. I don't want your comfort seven years too late. And so we're clear, there wasn't *someone else*, because you lost me the day you left. And a little more every day after that. Until finally I wasn't waiting for you to come back at all, I wasn't hoping and wondering and wishing, because I'd let you go. So, I'm sorry, because I know what it feels like to love someone who doesn't love you. But what we had is over. I'm with someone else now." And God, I wish he was here. No matter whether the physical part of our arrangement has an expiration date, when the chips are down, Rux is the man I turn to.

Jeremy swallows, pain in his eyes. "I understand. You have a relationship. A life. And I'm lucky that you were willing to disrupt it enough to give me a chance to be the father I should've been for Matty all these years. But I want you to know that if you change your mind, if you can remember what it was like between us, I'm ready to be the man you deserve. I'm ready for us to be the family we dreamed about having."

I don't know what to say, but it looks like Jeremy isn't expecting me to say anything. He takes a breath and looks around the kitchen.

"Hey, why don't I clean up from dinner and when Matty's out of the shower, I'll say good night then."

Chapter 21

Rux

"That fucker is working her. Right now," I growl, prowling back and forth in the too-small conference room Baxter and I commandeered for the few free minutes I've got pregame, restless energy building in me like a powder keg.

Greg's here to watch from the owner's box but stopped down to the locker room a few minutes ago. And after one look, he hauled me out, demanding to know what my problem was.

"Whoa, Rux, when you say 'working her' you don't mean—"

My hand is up, my finger shaking into the space between us. "Don't you even say it."

He visibly relaxes, walking a couple steps toward

me and knocking my hand out of the way to pull me in for a one-armed hug that ends with him messing up my hair.

"You had me worried there a second. I mean, I've seen you get worked up before but, damn, this"—he waves his hand all around in front of me—"is some next-level freak-out. I thought for sure… Never mind."

I gulp. "You thought what? You thought Cammy would be with him again?"

I don't like the look in his eyes. "Not while you guys are together. Even with whatever kind of friends-with-benefits thing you've got going, that's not how she is. If something is going to happen with Jeremy, she'll end it with you first."

Now I want to lay Baxter out. Because, "No shit, that's not how she is."

"Look, I know Julia hates his ass. I don't think that'll ever change. And the guy isn't winning any points with me. But I'm not entirely sure Cammy has ever gotten over Jeremy, okay? Julia says she has, but if you ever catch her talking about him when her guard is down, you can see that there's still something there."

Not possible. "He *abandoned* her."

"I know. But… What if he really has changed? Grown up in all the ways that matter?" He shrugs. "I agree, there's no excuse for what he did, and I hope she doesn't take him back. But what if he really has been trying to get his life together so that he'd have something to offer when he came home? Julia says this guy spent a year trying to get transferred to Chicago. That he took a serious pay cut to make it happen. What if, deep down, he's the one she wants?"

Suddenly all the energy that was ready to blow out of me in every different direction starts drawing inward, dragging me down until I drop into one of the chairs against the wall, my forearms catching on the spread of my knees feeling like the only thing keeping me from going through the floor.

"I don't want to lose her, man." The words feel like a confession ripped from the deepest, darkest, most secret part of my soul. Like I didn't even recognize it myself until just this moment.

"Come on, man, this is Cammy. You're not gonna lose her. I mean yeah, you'll lose the blowjobs, but that girl loves you."

I don't even want to hear him joke like that about her.

She loves me like a friend. It ought to be enough. But in this minute—fuck, I can almost see what it would be like if she loved me for real. Forever.

"Dude?"

I turn. Greg's brows buckle together, and I've got the sense he might be picking up on something I can barely admit to wanting myself.

"Rux, this thing between you guys, it's been great for you both. Some fun. Just what she needed. No responsibility, no expectation... Just the way you like it. But unless something fundamental has changed that I don't know about, you aren't a forever kind of guy. And ultimately, forever is what Cammy's been waiting for."

"But with *Jeremy*?"

"No idea, man. I'm not even sure Cammy does. I mean, hell, she's got your ass all over her every free minute you guys spend together. You're in her bed, with her kid. Probably cleaning out her refrigerator like it's your own. You're larger than life. And with you in front of her, I'm not sure if she can even see what she wants herself."

I swallow, my lungs feeling like they aren't working so great as I try to breathe through this feeling of being gutted.

"What are you saying? You think I should get out of the way?"

I'm waiting for him to give me a top volume *hell no*, and tell me to ride this out for as long as Cammy wants to give me. But I've got the uncomfortable sense that in this moment, Greg Baxter is more Cammy's brother-in-law than he is my wingman. And as much as I don't like it, I'm grateful knowing he's looking out for her when my mind is too clouded with my own selfish needs to see things clearly.

"I'm just saying, if you *know* you're not the right guy for her, maybe it's time to step aside so she has a chance to find the one who is."

Cammy

MATTY and I start the game curled up beneath the Slayers throw Rux gave us when the season started last year. Jeremy took off like he said he would and now it's just me and my boy, watching our favorite hockey player having an off game.

Rux has been in the box twice, missed what the commentators were calling two prime shots, and, like the rest of the team, can't seem to sync up with his line.

When the period ends, Matty gives me a pleading look, telling me Rux *needs* him.

"Sorry, buddy, we can watch the rest tomorrow." I pause the game and give my boy a squeeze before letting him up and then following him back to his room. He climbs into bed and I read a little *Fly Guy* before giving him a kiss and saying good night.

When I come back to the game, the second period is even worse than the first.

The Epics are all over our guys. Quinn O'Brian is tangled up with an opposing player against the boards, sticks clattering together as they fight it out for control of the puck. There's an opening, but Rux can't get there and misses the pass.

The look on his face in that moment guts me.

Three minutes later and he's in the box again, everyone talking about his failure to deliver. How they'd had high hopes for the rivalry with the Epics pushing our players to perform better, but instead we're falling apart.

I'm on the edge of my seat, waiting for the game to turn around. But it doesn't happen, and by the end I can barely stand to watch the interviews.

It takes longer than usual for Rux to call, but finally he does and I feel like I can breathe again.

"Hey, how are you?" I ask quietly.

"Had better games, that's for damn sure. Tell me you didn't watch the whole thing."

I debate lying for a second, but he cuts into my thoughts with a rough laugh.

"Course you did."

"What can I say, you've got a fan."

I hear him take a deep breath through the line and imagine him climbing into his car. "You coming over?"

There's a beat of silence, and then— "I wish. But I'm already home. I've got a meeting with the coach early tomorrow, and I'm not much company after tonight."

"Oh sure. Rest. But… umm… okay, I don't want to keep you when I know you're tired, but about Jeremy and what you texted when you left?"

Again there's that barest hesitation and I jump into silence before he has a chance to answer. "It doesn't matter how he feels. He's not the one I want."

"Cammy, you know… it would be okay if he was."

I blink, staring down at the phone like it just lied to me. Like there is no way the man on the other end actually said what I just heard. I know this thing between us isn't forever, but… *It would be okay?*

After a few more seconds of my stunned silence, he adds, "Sorry to do this, but I'm about to fall asleep. Talk to you later, Sunshine."

"Oh, okay, right. Um… good night, Rux."

Chapter 22

Rux

The meetings with the coaches go about as you'd expect with the game we had. The season's winding down and while it doesn't look good for playoffs this year, no one is ready to give up. Morning skate is brutal, but it's what I need to keep from doing what I spent the entire damn night talking myself out of—driving over to Cammy's place and begging her to let me hold her. Telling her I didn't mean what I said. That there would be nothing okay about it if she decided Jeremy was the man for her.

But I can't do that. And it's not because I wouldn't put a ring on Cammy's finger and make Matty my own in a hot second if I thought it was the right thing. It's that I know she deserves better and so I won't.

We run double drills, and then I stay even longer. I push harder. Dig deeper. I'm not going to let Cammy down. And I'm not going to let this team down either.

By the time I'm done, I can barely drag myself off the ice. As I start taking off my skates, O'Brian comes in with Vassar and Popov from weights.

Just the man I'm waiting for. "O'Brian, what have you got going on this afternoon?"

"Inner city arts program. You?"

"Nada. My day got canceled. Flooding at the convention center or something." I hate myself for what I'm about to do, but I do it anyway. "Want me to take yours? Give you a night off?"

O'Brian's brows shoot up, a smile spreading across his face. We all feel good about the charity work we do with the team, but nobody turns down the chance for a night off. Hell, except me, apparently.

But if I'm booked, then I won't be showing up at Cammy's place, building Legos with Matty and stealing kisses from his mom when he goes to bed. I won't be holding her in my arms while we watch *Oak Island*, when I need to be letting her go so she has a chance to find the kind of forever she deserves.

Cammy

"I'M TELLING YOU, these guys are at the mercy of the team," Julia assures me through the line. She's in LA tonight but had a few free minutes before whatever dinner or event she's got lined up. "PR asks them to do something, they need to do it."

"Okay, I get that, but Julia, this is the third time in a week and a half. And maybe that doesn't seem like a lot when these guys are traveling and as busy as they are, but this is Rux. I'm telling you, something's off."

There's some shuffling from the other end of the line, and I'm pretty sure it's Greg in the background, but I can't make out what he's saying. Julia tells him to give her another minute, and then she's back, a new concern behind her words. "You haven't seen Rux in a week and a half?"

I blow a curl from my eyes and throw up my hand in frustration even though she's not here to see it. "No. I mean, *yes*, I've seen him. But it's only been a couple times, and just when Matty is around. Like maybe, he's not dodging *us*. He's just dodging *me*."

"No. No way."

I like that flat-out refusal in accepting something so obviously impossible. I want to wrap myself up in it, but... I know better. I know Rux. And something's going on with him.

I want to blame it on whatever happened that night when Jeremy followed him out, but there was something before that. More than the fact that he wasn't dirty-talking my ear off every night, were the moments when he was too quiet. When I'd see him watching Matty with a pained look in his eyes. I asked if he was okay, and he'd snap back to the same old Rux—throwing out some crazy suggestion that no one could say no to.

What's going on with him?

"Do you think it's possible this doesn't have anything to do with you at all? I mean, with the way the season has been going, he's dealing with some pressure, right?"

Walking back to the kitchen, I open cabinets, close them with a sigh. "He is. I know."

And if that's what it is, I completely understand. I just wish I could do something to make it better, the way he makes everything better for me.

"Hey, Cammy," Julia says gently. "Do you want me to ask Greg?"

It's tempting, but no way am I going to ask my sister to pump my sort-of-boyfriend's best friend for information about my relationship. "Thanks, but I'll talk to him myself."

That's what we do.

We talk to each other about everything. Almost everything.

. . .

"RUX!" Matty squeals, running across the living room as our favorite Slayer closes the door behind him.

Rux gives him a big bear hug before walking over to me and dropping a kiss at the top of my head. One arm pulls me in to his side and, God, he smells so good. And he looks even better, tall and broad in navy athletic pants and a gray hoodie, cheeks a little red from the wind blowing in off the lake today.

"How you doing, Sunshine?"

So much better now that he's here. I don't know why, but all day I've been worried that he wouldn't come.

"I'm doing great. Finished work an hour early. Got the supplies for Matty's project from the dollar store and managed to knock out some yoga."

That warm smile I love so much spreads wider. "Badass."

Matty skids up to him, shaking his head. "She only did the thirty-minute workout."

Rux's eyes crinkle at the corners, and then we're all laughing together and it feels so normal. So right. It feels like the kind of moment you want again and again and again. Like the kind of moment you want to keep having forever.

Matty leads Rux to the fridge, proudly pointing out the fresh batch of carrot cake cupcakes we made. Rux makes all the appropriate noises, *ooh*ing and *ahh*ing about them. But what I love best is that it's not just for Matty's benefit. This is a man who says what's on his mind and wears his feelings on his sleeve. And he loves carrot cake.

After he carefully peels one and then basically inhales it, we all settle into the living room to catch up on the day.

Matty's head pops up and he grabs my phone off the table to check the time. "Mom, Teddy's parents are going to be here in ten minutes."

I force myself to keep my eyes on my boy rather than dissect Rux's every blink and swallow at the realization we're going to be alone tonight after all.

I'm being silly. I know it.

The minute the door closes, this man is going to have me backed up against it, devouring my mouth in that ravenous way of his. His hands will be roaming my body with that wildfire touch. And then later when it's just the two of us in bed, his big arms holding me against him, I'll tell him about my unfounded fears.

He'll kiss me again and tell me he's not going anywhere.

"Why don't you grab your bag from your room and put it by the door." I smile as Matty darts off.

Still caught up in that fantasy, I turn to Rux... and my heart sinks. His strained expression is unmistakable.

I'm not imagining it.

"Where's Matty heading?" he asks, all his usual easygoing replaced by the kind of uncomfortable that has dread spooling through my belly.

"Sleepover."

It's almost painful to see Rux sit back and force a smile to his lips. To pretend that this isn't a turn of events he'd rather not have seen or faced. It feels like something inside me is breaking, and if I'm not careful, I'll betray everything I've been trying to hide.

Before I do something stupid like start to cry in front of him, I make an excuse about double-checking that Matty packed his toothbrush and escape to the other room.

Once I'm out of sight, I close my eyes and press my hand to my aching heart. Swallow past the rise of emotion in my throat and fight to keep the tears at bay.

It takes a minute to get my head straight, but I'm strong.

When Matty steps out of his room, backpack slung over his shoulder and a bright smile on his face, I'm ready to return it with my own.

"You excited, buddy?"

He's practically bouncing where he stands as he nods enthusiastically.

A few minutes later I'm blowing him a kiss and waving as he leaves with Teddy's family.

Stepping back into the apartment, I find Rux waiting for me. He's on his feet, leaning against the back of the couch.

This is it.

We're alone. But instead of Rux stalking me across the room and using his body to pin me to the door, he's staring at his shoes.

I move into the open spot beside him and let my hand rest on his.

His head drops low and he sighs.

"There are rumors of a trade."

My chest goes tight as I grip his hand tighter. "What? When?"

Finally his eyes meet mine. "I have no idea. Management isn't talking, but that doesn't mean anything."

I know from Julia and being around this team for so long, that sometimes a player is the last to know, and sometimes a player will have trade rumors floating around them for years without ever amounting to anything.

"Have there been rumors about you before?"

He shakes his head. "They're from reliable sources. Julia was going to call you, but I told her I was on my way over."

I try to pull a breath, but my lungs don't want to work.

"It was just a couple of games," I offer weakly, like somehow my words could impact actions potentially already in motion.

"Important games. The ones where they've been watching to see how I would perform."

This can't be happening. The Slayers would never let Rux go. They can't. He loves Chicago. He loves this team.

No wonder he's been acting strange lately.

"Do *you* think you're going?" I ask quietly.

"Honest to God, I have no idea." Then after a long breath, he shakes his head. "Look, Cammy. There's a lot of uncertainty in my life right now. Even if I don't get traded, the adjustments with the team—"

"It's a lot," I whisper, seeing the truth of it in his apology-filled eyes. I hate what comes next, but I need to be the one to say it. "Even without adding a friends-with-benefits package into the mix and the feelings that may or may not go along with it."

The breath that leaves his chest is relieved, if a little uneven. When our eyes meet, I try to smile and even if it doesn't work very well, for once, Rux doesn't point it out.

Taking my hand in his, he pulls it into his lap. "I

don't want to lose you, Cammy. I don't want to lose Matty."

"You won't," I promise, blinking at the tears threatening to fall.

"So, friends?" he asks, pulling me in front of him and looping his arms around my waist.

It's not the kind of stance we would have found ourselves in before all of this started, and I'm guessing it's one we won't revisit going forward. But in this minute, I can still rest my hand against the solid planes of his chest, I can still brush the stubble of his cheek with my thumb.

"Of course. Friends," I say, quietly enough I'm hoping he can't hear the way I struggle to say it. "Always."

His eyes close in what must be relief. He turns into my palm and kisses the sensitive skin, making my heart ache all the more.

A minute passes, but neither of us move. Neither pulls away.

I don't know what his reason is. Comfort probably. Reassurance.

Mine is more that I can't seem to make myself let go, that a part of me wants to hold him forever. Sliding my hand up his chest, I step in closer between his legs and wrap my arms around his neck.

The arms at my waist tighten and then one slides

up my back, holding me close and closer. It's so good, so warm, so safe, I never want to leave. His hand smooths over my hair and cups the back of my neck.

He pulls back and lets his eyes run over my features, ending at my mouth.

I can practically feel the echoes of his kisses.

His eyes come back to mine, and as if by unspoken agreement we lean in for one last kiss.

I tremble against him, breathe him in as he breathes me.

One last time, my fingers thread through his hair.

I need to let him go. It's time. Past.

The breath between us changes, the seconds stretch and pull, the awareness builds and then with one desperate look, snaps. Rux kisses me hard, crushing his mouth to mine and groaning my name.

Yes.

Our bodies can't get close enough. I'll never have enough.

We move through the apartment blind.

"One last time," I whisper when he lays me back on the bed.

Reaching over his shoulder, he fists the back of his shirt and pulls it over his head in a move I will never get tired of. "One last time."

We shuck our clothes, kicking and tossing them

aside, and come back together in a desperate, hungry clash of lips and teeth and tongues.

"Sunshine," he growls against my neck, my breasts. My fingers thread through his hair, holding him against me as he circles my nipple with his tongue, then draws it into the wet heat of his mouth.

"Need you, Rux," I gasp, pulling at his shoulders and arms as his firm grip urges my hips into the press of his.

Dark eyes meet mine, burning and intense. "This isn't goodbye. You know that, right?"

He's wrong. This is goodbye to a dream that I'd only just started to believe in. To a hope that had quietly, stealthily wound its way into my heart. It's goodbye to the idea that I might have finally found the one man I could trust with my whole heart again. That I could let myself love completely and know that, with him, I would be safe.

Stroking the side of his face, I shake my head. "It's not goodbye to us, but... it's goodbye to something that was pretty good, right?"

Our eyes hold, and for a moment he looks pained. But in a blink whatever I thought I was seeing is gone, replaced by my best friend's smile. "So good."

And when I feel like I might be about to cry, I force a smile instead and joke lightly, "So how about you give me something to remember you by."

Rux drops his forehead against my chest with a gruff laugh and then peers up at me with an arched brow. The mischief I love shines in his eyes. "Just one thing to remember me by?"

This guy. My smile stretches wide. "One thing. Two. Whatever you can manage."

And then my big strong hockey-playing stud is back, prowling up my body, using his to box me in. "Oh, I can manage more than two."

Chapter 23

Rux

I shouldn't have done it.

I should have told her what was happening with the trade rumors, waved my limp fucking excuse around, kissed the top of her head and walked out. But when she looked up at me, it was right there in her eyes.

One more time.

She joked about me giving her something to remember me by. Yeah, I wanted that too. I wanted to give her so much to remember me by that she won't be able to think about sex without practically moaning my name.

I want the next sorry fuck who tries to put a hand on her—

"Rux, you're growling," Cammy pants, her hand on my bare chest as I sink into her full length, shift my hips in that way that makes her lips part and her breath catch.

—to be so inferior to me that a hand is *all* he ever gets to put on her.

"Oh God... I can't..."

She *can*. I'd get her there faster if I was behind her, but I won't give up being with her like this, face to face. So I dig deep—

"Mmmm... *again*."

Her wish is my command.

"Rux!" And then she's there, giving me my personal best for number of times getting her off. But this time, I can't hold off. This time when our eyes meet and her body comes hard around mine, I let her take me with her. I follow her over the edge, holding on to that contact, that bond, that feeling of connection on a level I shouldn't have with this girl, but will hold close to my heart for the rest of my days.

Minutes later, her head is resting on my shoulder, hand over my heart.

How am I going to give her up?

She takes in an even breath, and then another. And when she peers up at me, my heart breaks.

"I know you have too much going on right now. And the last thing you need is something edging its way toward a relationship when it wasn't supposed to go like that. But maybe, it doesn't have to be the *end*." She bites her lip, barely meeting my eyes. "Maybe just once in a while, if the mood strikes us, maybe we could—"

"No." Jesus, one word has never cost me so much. "Cammy, we can't. As insanely good as this feels." Better than anything I've ever had in my life. Especially the part where I hold her after. "It isn't what either of us needs right now."

It's almost the truth. It's the best I can do for her.

The nod she gives me is tight against my chest, and I know it's not what she wanted to hear. That I'm hurting her feelings, but I need to do the right thing here.

Another breath, this one deep and full, and she sits, looking at me with a smile. "You're right. I know you are."

She leans down and presses a soft kiss to my lips, and when she sits back, she's not mine anymore.

Cammy

RUX HAD an out-of-town game the next day and was back the day after. He stopped by when Matty was around, and if I'd been worried about things being weird or different between us, I shouldn't have. Rux came in like he always does, full of energy and excitement. An easy kiss at the top of my head and that brief one-armed hug that had always felt perfect, at least up until the time when I discovered how good the two-armed or even full-bodied varieties could be.

It was normal.

It was *harder* than I expected, simply for how seamlessly Rux slipped back into the role of just friends.

I should have been grateful. I mean, what kind of jerk wants to see someone they care about suffer? I don't. Seeing Rux unhappy is almost as bad as seeing my boy in pain.

And the rational part of my brain knows that this ease is the best thing that could've happened. For me, for Rux, and most importantly for Matty.

But maybe some small ugly part of me wouldn't mind an hour of things not being quite so comfortable between us. A small sign that on some level, he misses being with me the way I miss being with him.

But no.

It was just that easy for him to let me go.

Just like it had been for Jeremy.

So we hung out. We goofed around. And then Rux left for a five-day road trip.

And as much as I don't like it, as much as I miss

him, I have to admit that the break is probably what we need so I can get myself back on track, and reset my emotions to just friends.

Only three days in and I'm still not sleeping. I keep thinking about what it was like between us. How right it felt in his arms. The way he'd look at me when he came over after his games. How he loved staying home with me. The way he couldn't get enough of my son.

How I could have sworn he was falling.

"Are you sick?" Matty's staring at me from across the breakfast table and I'm pretty sure the kid doesn't mean heartsick.

"No, honey. Just a little tired today. I'll be fine," I assure with the smile I can always find for him.

"If you want, I can stay here and take care of you."

That hyper-vigilant part of me that's constantly on alert about this little boy's happiness comes on line. "You don't want to go to your dad's?"

"No! I want to see Dad. But I like to be here too. Maybe this time he could come over here and hang out with us... All my toys are here, and I want to show him. Please, Mom?"

Seriously, the last thing I need right now is Jeremy underfoot. But when I look into my son's pleading face, I can't say no.

"How about we check with your dad and see if he has any plans."

Matty shakes his head like I have no idea, like I've never met this guy before.

"No way. Dad loves to come over here. Says hanging out with you is almost as much fun as hanging out with me."

Crossing my arms, I nod. "Still, let me call him and see."

An hour and a half later, I'm on my fourth cup of coffee and Jeremy is unloading a new set of Play-Doh on the kitchen counter.

Matty isn't usually into that stuff so much, but the way he's acting now, you'd think it was the only thing he asked for for Christmas.

I'm about to head into the living room and check my email, when Jeremy asks if I want to get in on the build. Again, it's those eyes from my boy that have me saying yes when I really want to say no. And I'll admit, it turns out to be fun. Jeremy's always been a creative guy, and when applied to Play-Doh and dinosaurs I can see why Matty has fun.

But I can't help compare him to Rux and the way he interacts with Matty. Definitely a more physical play —even when they're building Legos, Rux's arms are always flying out from his sides, mimicking attacking forces, or maybe a tornado. His world-building is active with wild stories and crazy characters.

Jeremy's is quiet, reserved. Concentrated on design and layout. There's a backstory, but while Rux is building a battleground to play on, Jeremy is building one suitable for display.

I have a small ball of dough I gave up on forming about two minutes in. Fatigue is weighing on me, and when I can't take it any longer, I give Jeremy a pleading look.

"Hey, I didn't really sleep well last night." Or the night before. "Any chance you guys would be good on your own while I lie down?"

"Absolutely," he encourages. "Go get some shut-eye. Matty and I'll finish our prehistoric lava monster."

It's an offer I can't refuse. And after dropping a kiss on Matty's cheek I head back into the seclusion of my room.

No text from Rux.

I set the alarm on my phone for forty-five minutes and crawl into bed. Just a quick nap and I'll be good to go.

Rux

I MADE it as long as I could. But if I don't talk to Cammy in the next five minutes I'm going to lose my shit.

"Space and time" sucks.

I hate it. And yeah, I get that with the kinds of changes we're going through, it's supposed to be a good thing. But I've been about ready to crawl out of my skin not texting just to see how she's doing. How her morning is. What she had for lunch. How she slept.

Better than me, I hope.

I'm walking in through the hotel lobby after practice and meetings this afternoon. I'm anxious as fuck about the game tonight. The last few we've been playing better, but something's still missing. Something more than the woman I keep telling myself not to want.

Pulling out my phone, I nod to a couple of guys wearing Slayers jerseys watching me from the coffee stand. One of our trainers is talking up some chick next to the restaurant. Perfect, I can call with a blow-by-blow account for an excuse. She'll love it.

I wait for the line to connect, for that missing *something* in my chest to fill in at the sound of her voice, Matty in the background chirping out updates on drama at school or his Lego city.

"Rux!"

I pull the phone back, checking to make sure I dialed Cammy's number and not Matty's.

"Hey, little man, what are you doing with your mom's phone?" I ask, imagining him at the kitchen table with an action figure and Cammy at the counter starting on dinner.

"My mom and dad are napping right now."

I'm a guy known for my lightning-fast reflexes. For snap decisions that make or break a game. That means processing information at the speed of a flying puck.

But this?

The skin across my cheeks feels funny and my voice doesn't sound like my own when I choke out the only word I can manage, "*What?*"

"Sleeping. I guess, maybe, they didn't get enough sleep last night," he tells me casually in that throaty little voice I love.

Trainer forgotten, I turn where I am and start walking back toward the street. Toward the airport or maybe the highway.

Everything inside me demands action. Retribution. An ass-kicking. Me on my knees in front of Cammy begging her to give me another chance. Telling her I fucked up. I didn't mean it.

Good enough for her or not, *I don't want her to pick him.*

If she deserves more security in her future than I

can give her, then she sure as fuck deserves more than the guy who abandoned her seven years ago!

Matty's still chatting. He sounds almost amused.

And why wouldn't he be? He's seven. And his mother and father are together in the way people who are part of a family are together.

He's probably elated.

I should be. It's why I ripped my heart out and let his mother go. So she would have the clarity to make this kind of choice.

He's talking about dinosaurs and Play-Doh now, and how his dad is really good at building. How he showed him how to do some of it, but Matty didn't think his was as good.

"No way, Matty. I bet yours is the best of them all."

I should get off the phone. Let Matty get back to his family. But even knowing that Cammy and Jeremy—

Fuck!

I can't make myself hang up.

More than ever, I feel the need to hold on. To listen to every word that Matty is telling me about how the orange and the green got too mixed up and couldn't be separated. And how his dad was really good at making stuff but didn't know how to wreck it the way I did.

This kid has no idea how right he is. I know how to wreck things, whether I mean to or not.

"Okay, Rux, my dad's getting up now. I have to go."

Jesus, the visual running through my head right now makes me sick. Jeremy, with his perfect pretty-boy hair sticking up like mine does after Cammy's had her fingers in it for an hour. Some smug, satisfied look on his face as he staggers out of her bedroom... Maybe giving her a few minutes to get herself put back together before she rejoins her son.

"I'll talk to you later, Matty."

"Oh, Rux?"

I come to a stop halfway down the block and sit on the curb. "Yeah?"

"Have a good game tonight," he says, and that awesome smile coming through the line breaks my heart.

"Thanks, buddy. I will."

But the team we're up against? Something tells me, they're not gonna have a good game.

Chapter 24

Cammy

I wake, disoriented, coming out of a sleep so deep and hard I'm shaky as I push-up to sit. The light coming in from behind the blinds seems wrong.

It takes me a minute to remember it's not morning and I haven't just slept the night through. I only closed my eyes for a nap, I set my alarm, but— Where's my phone?

Matty's little laugh drifts in from beyond my door, and I smile. I can practically see him out there, playing with Rux, and—

I stumble as my brain catches up.

Not Rux, I'm reminded as my hand reaches the cold metal of the knob.

Jeremy.

That's right.

My heart deflates a little, and again I glance around for my phone. Has Rux called, texted?

But another sweeping glance of the room doesn't reveal anything, and I figure I'll come back for it later. First, I want to check on Matty.

Stepping out into the hallway, I'm greeted by my little boy rocketing toward me for hug. Beyond, Jeremy's sitting on the couch, looking a bit rumpled himself.

"Mom, you slept forever! Your alarm was going off, and Dad said maybe we should let you rest, so I went in and took your phone."

Is that so? My eyes shift between my son and his father who's rubbing the back of his neck, giving me an uneasy smile.

"I hope it's okay. You looked exhausted and, since I was here, I figured why not let you sleep."

I don't want to make a big deal of it now, but I'll talk to Matty about taking my phone in future.

"We played Play-Doh forever! Dad didn't want dinosaurs to destroy their new house, so we put *Sarah's Wrap* over it and then played a board game. And then we put on a show, but he was tired too and fell asleep while we were watching. And I made this picture for

Rux, so he can take it with him when he goes on road trips. I think he misses us when he's gone."

The flood of information coming at me at lightning speed starts to process and I rub my hand over Matty's hair.

"I bet Rux would love that picture." I lean down and give him a hug. "Show it to me?"

Proudly, he leads me over to the coffee table, and the single sheet of paper that has my heart aching and emotion crawling up my throat.

"Oh, he's going to love this," I say, hoping Matty can't hear the tremor in my voice. No tears, damn it.

The picture is clearly of Rux in his Slayers gear, little lines beneath his feet indicating skates. Close beside him is a figure with blond hair and blue eyes, a slight variation on the picture he draws of me every time. And at his other side is Matty's small form smiling wide, holding his hand.

Matty turns back to his dad. "You and Rux aren't that good of friends yet, so this picture is just us. But the next one I make, you can be in."

Jeremy's smile doesn't falter, but I've known this man since he was a boy. And though he's doing a pretty good job of covering it up, I catch the smallest flinch of hurt.

"Can't wait, kiddo."

Matty lets me take a picture of his drawing, and then dashes back to his room to put it in a safe place for the next time he sees Rux.

I turn to Jeremy, wanting to say something reassuring. But he holds his hand up, shaking his head.

"I get it. Rux has been a part of his life for years longer than I've been back. But I'm hoping in time Matty will see me as much a part of his family as him."

Something about the way he says it triggers another emotional response. Turning toward the windows, I try to keep the heartbreak and hurt from my face.

But just like my history with Jeremy lets me see things others might not, his with me does the same.

Coming up behind me, he rests his hand on my shoulder.

"Hey, that's the second time in five minutes you looked like you might cry. And I'm thinking about the fact that you weren't sleeping. Everything okay? With you and Rux, I mean?"

I nod tightly, not trusting my voice. And honestly Jeremy is the last person I want to talk about Rux to. But he's not ready to leave it alone.

"Something happen with you guys?"

Before I have to answer, Matty is skidding back

into the room, handful of action figures gripped tight in his fist. "For with the Play-Doh!"

I can't help but smile, all that threatening emotion evaporating beneath my son's excitement. At least enough to keep it from spilling over in front of these two. "You know the best part of building an awesome model is tearing it down."

Jeremy lets out a sigh. "Yeah, I'm getting that sense. Come and see it before the troops take over."

By the time he leaves, I've missed my window for Rux to call, or for me to call him.

He'll be getting ready for the game, and considering what he said about distractions, I've been working very hard not to be one. So instead, I fire off a quick text, wishing him a good game.

I want to tell him I'll be up later, that he could call when the game is over… if he wants to talk.

I wouldn't have thought twice about it a month ago or even six. But now it seems needy. Pushy. Desperate.

And maybe that's because I know the truth. I'm all of those things.

I'm aching to talk to him, to hear his voice. His laugh.

To know how he felt about his game and if he's heard anything more about a trade.

But Rux ended what was happening between us because it was too much. He needed some breathing room. And I'm going to give it to him.

———

Rux

I GET HER TEXT AND...*DAMN*.

She's wishing me luck in the game.

Not casually mentioning that in less than a week, things are going so well with Jeremy, that in addition to letting him keep her up all night, they're napping together while Matty's there.

The air in my lungs turns to glass.

"Whoa, man." O'Brian's in front of me, a look of concern in his eyes as he looks from my phone back to my face. "That thing sounds like it's about to bust."

My knuckles are white wrapped around the device, but the screen is still lit up with Cammy's text.

"Everything okay there?" he asks quietly, not trying to draw attention. He's a good kid, and after the way I've been playing, he's probably wondering what my impending meltdown means for the game tonight.

"It's all good. The way it's supposed to be." I think. I hope.

Fine, maybe I *don't* hope. Because I'm a jealous, selfish dick.

He nods. Shakes his head. Shrugs. "Don't take this the wrong way, but doesn't really look that way."

"I'll have my shit together for the game. I'm fine." I rake a hand through my hair. "Just getting used to things being different with Cammy, that's all."

"She's texting you. That's good. Or——" He takes an uneasy step back, wincing as he asks, "Is that not good?"

I can see the discomfort on his face. "What, you think I'm trying to *shake her*? Cammy Wesley. Baxter's little-sister-in-law."

"Hell, I don't know what to think with the way you're glaring at that thing. And seriously, at this point, I'm not sure anyone around here is thinking of her as Baxter's anything." His hands come up before I have a chance to react. "Not because of his status on the team either. Just pretty sure if anyone thinks of her as anyone's… it's yours."

Mine.

I drop back against the wall and shake my head. "I don't think that's going to stick."

"You guys break up?"

Yes? No? Is it really breaking up when you go back to being friends after being friends with benefits?

"She's getting back with Matty's dad. We're still friends."

He blinks at me a minute. Then looks around before stepping in closer. "Rux, I'm sorry, man. And it doesn't take any more than looking at you to know you need to vent off some... feelings. But this is serious. People are watching. What you do tonight matters. You hear what I'm saying?"

I nod. That talk of trades isn't going away. I need to play with my head in the game, not like some jealous torqued-off boyfriend. Because even if I'm not the guy who gets Cammy forever, I don't want to leave her and Matty. "I've got this."

"I know you do. We're going to be unstoppable out there. And this shit you've got in your head right now?"

Feels more like my heart than my head, but I'm not going to argue with him.

"*Use it.* But be smart about how you do, right?" He claps a hand on my shoulder and heads for the ice.

Closing my eyes, I breathe through my nose. Think about the plays. The game. The opposing players and everything I know about them.

I think about those soft blue eyes looking up at me the last time I was inside— *No.*

Refocusing, I think about what the assistant coach talked about after morning skate. About Matty waking up with his dad and mom coming out of Cammy's room— My fist bangs back into the wall.

My time is up. I need to get my head in the game. I need to play like I'm part of this winning team and not some wash-up waiting on getting traded.

I hit the ice hard. Doesn't bother me that I'm not starting. If I were the one making the decisions, after the last couple of games, I'm not sure I'd play me at all.

But tonight's different. It's not like the last few games.

Tonight, my focus is laser sharp. There's nothing but the puck and a bunch of assholes who want to keep it from me... And every single one of them looks like Jeremy Levenson.

Cammy

RUX IS ON FIRE. The commentators can't stop talking about him, speculating over what it is that changed between the last game and this one.

It's like he took charge of the ice and everyone fell into line. Everyone from our team, that is.

The opponents? They can't catch their breath.

They can't keep up. And God forbid anyone get in his way… They feel it.

He's playing hard. And he's playing smart. And while each hit he delivers has my knees tucking tighter into my chest and the breath punching from my lungs —they're good hits. Solid plays. And he's putting the Slayers solidly in the lead.

This is how Rux plays when he isn't distracted, when he's able to clear his head and bring his focus back to the game.

I've seen Rux play hard before. But this is something different. This is intense, and amazing. And a little bit terrifying. This is the man I love, fighting to stay on the team *he loves*.

Matty looked like he might never forgive me when I told him he needed to go to bed after the second period, but five minutes into the third, and I know I made the right choice. The other team has had it with Rux and is starting to come back, retaliating with cheap shots and hits that fall further over the line each time.

And then it happens, that high stick from number twelve coming down in a slash.

My breath stalls in my lungs, and I'm off the couch, stumbling toward the TV like there's something I can do. Like I can stop the flow of blood on the ice or the look of murder in Rux's eyes.

Players from both sides are coming at each other, while the refs struggle to regain control. Then Quinn O'Brian is there, helping Rux to his feet and blocking him with his body when Rux turns back to the fray.

The camera cuts away when he gets to the bench, and my heart stops. Who cares about the stupid game? The only thing that matters to me right now is the man who just left it.

My phone pings with a message from Julia telling me he's fine and she's betting Rux is back on the ice in the next five minutes.

Me: Maybe he shouldn't go back out?

Julia: LOL not my call, Sis.

Julia: It's a rough game. They're used to this. And from the look in Rux's eyes skating off, something tells me he's more than ready to get back on.

I watch the rest of the game, texting back and forth with my sister. She was right, Rux is back in for the last five. And the hit number twelve takes from Vaughn when he gets out of the penalty box sends him sailing. Hard. It's legal. And definitely intended to cut Rux off before he had the chance to retaliate on his own.

When the game is through, I text asking if he's okay before I can talk myself out of it.

He's probably got someone looking at his mouth.

There are interviews and who knows what else after the game. But I'm hoping he'll call if he gets a minute.

But when I hear from him, it's just a text telling me he's fine and that I should get some sleep.

Translation: He's not calling.

Which is fine. Except then I can't stop myself from wondering… what he's doing to burn off all that aggression from tonight's game.

Chapter 25

Rux

$\mathcal{I}$ got home late last night, and it felt weird walking into my apartment without calling Cammy or stopping over. But I'm self-aware enough to recognize that no way am I in a place where I can handle calling at two a.m. and maybe hearing Jeremy in the background, rumbling sleepily—or worse, not so sleepily—about who's on the phone.

I'll get there, maybe. Or maybe I'll just stop calling in the middle of the night. I'll keep my calls and visits —like today's—restricted to the hours when Matty's awake.

I rake a hand through my hair, feeling agitated and out of sorts.

What if Jeremy is here? What if he's moving in?

I feel like I'm going to puke. What if she marries him?

I plant my hand against the wall beside the door and hang my head, trying to catch my breath.

I don't want to think about Cammy dressed in white and looking into fucking Jeremy's eyes while she vows to love him for the rest of her life.

One breath becomes two, and then two becomes three.

I need to get my shit together. Get my game face on. Just not the one where I'm visualizing Cammy's ex in place of all the opposing players and giving myself free rein to vent my aggressions when they try to take something from me I don't want them to have.

The door creaks open and I catch a little blue eye going wide at the sight of me.

Times's up.

"I told you he was out there!" Matty calls back to his mom as the door swings wide and my favorite kid in the world bounces from foot to foot.

"Hey buddy, how you doing?" I ask, stepping into the apartment because as much as I know he wants to, Matty's very good about not leaving the apartment by even a foot without his mom right there.

Little arms with the strength of a man lock around me as he starts rambling. "You were awesome, Rux. I watched part of all your games and then I got to see the end of some but not all. My mom didn't want me to worry about you getting hurt, but Billy Felton had it on YouTube and so I saw it anyway and you looked really mad. I bet that number twelve guy was scared of you. Is your mouth okay? Can I touch it? Does it hurt? Do you need some ice? When's your—"

"Matty," Cammy gently interrupts, wiping her hands on a dishtowel and then tucking the end into the pocket of her jeans, "let him catch his breath."

Matty pinches his lips together and peers up at me like he couldn't wait to see me again.

I can't bring myself to meet Cammy's eyes because I'm a total pussy and not ready for what I might see in them. So instead, I lean down, take a big, exaggerated breath and let it out in a noisy whistle that has him giggling and shaking his head at me like a mini version of his mom.

"Whew, think I finally caught it."

Matty smiles and I rub his mop of hair before bracing to look around. The space looks the same. It feels the same. No half-dead ficus plants. No unpacked cardboard boxes stacked in the corner. Not even a fresh pile of masculine junk accumulated on the coffee table.

No signs of a new, probably permanent occupant.

Okay, so maybe I can breathe.

"Mom didn't think you were coming over today."

"No?" I look from Matty's earnest face to Cammy's suddenly anxious one, a feeling of sinking dread moving through me. I should have called. Checked that it was okay.

"I told her you'd be here. But she told me you might be too busy and if you couldn't come, I shouldn't take it personally."

She's shaking her head, wringing her hands together as she peers across the open space between us. "Since I hadn't talked to you, I wasn't sure if you were still..."

She takes a breath and gives me a helpless look.

I let out a laugh I'm not totally feeling and make a mental note that I better start checking in before I show up here. "I said I'd come by, so—"

"I'm glad you did," she rushes, her hand moving through the air in an awkward wave that makes me want to pull her into my arms and hold her close. Instead, I keep my feet planted where they are as she adds, "We are."

Matty drags me back into the kitchen so I can check out the fridge. They made me banana muffins and after being challenged to see if I could eat the whole cupcake in one bite—umm, yes—Matty darts off to get something for me from his room.

Wiping my mouth on one of the thin napkins from

the metal dispenser on the kitchen table, I look up to find Cammy hovering at the kitchen doorway.

Christ, she's so fucking pretty, and all I want to do is haul her into my arms and hold her. I want her arms around me. Her tits squished up soft against my chest, her head against my heart.

"Thanks for the muffin."

"Matty wanted to make them for you."

Matty. Not her.

I look down at the floor around my feet, hating this tension sitting in the space between us.

From the first day I met this girl it was nothing but easy between us. Nothing but fun and relaxed and right. And now we can't even talk about a fucking muffin.

She takes a step toward me and my heart kicks, but then she stops. Her hands landing on the back of her kitchen chair.

"You looked good playing. Kind of intense."

"Yeah, good win."

Her hands coast over the back of the chair in a move that's almost restless, and I can't help thinking about the way her hands felt moving over me. How she'd let me rest my head in her lap while she played with my hair, giving me that gentle touch and sweet affection.

"You seemed kind of... different. Is everything okay?"

"Yeah, I just found my focus. Rhythm. Groove. Whatever."

"Are your coaches happy? Have you heard anything more about trades?"

Yeah, I've heard plenty. But at this point it's impossible to filter out the rumors from the truth. "Nothing solid."

I don't have an answer about the coaches. I don't really want to tell her that Coach Adkins said I looked like a psychopath out there those last two games.

"Does it hurt?" she asks quietly, her hand coming up and stroking my jaw just below the healing cut. And that touch, Jesus, I didn't even realize I'd been closing the space between us until she reached up and feathered her fingertips over my skin.

My hand closes around her wrist, holding her where she is. I close my eyes and feel that soft, gentle touch. Resisting the urge to dip my head so I can draw her fingers into my mouth.

"Rux?" My name is barely a whisper, but there's no missing the uncertainty behind it.

Giving in to one stroke of my thumb over her wrist, my eyes flip open and I smile. "It doesn't hurt. I'm fine."

I've moved her hand from my lips, but I haven't let her go. If she pulls away, I will. But for just this minute she doesn't seem to notice the way we're still connected.

I shouldn't be doing this. I shouldn't be standing alone with her in this kitchen or touching her like she's still mine. I shouldn't be staring into those bottomless blue eyes and asking myself what would happen if I pulled her closer. Let our bodies align the way it feels so good to do. Tip her head back until her lips part and I can sink—

"Rux, I made this for you," Matty says, rounding the corner, his eyes lowered to the sheet of paper he's holding in his hands.

Cammy and I step away from each other, and while I can't wait to see what this guy made for me, I'm aching to pull her back. To slip my fingers through hers. To pull her into my chest as we look over the latest masterpiece together.

Instead, I drop into a kitchen chair and wave him over to show me what he's done.

Instead of handing me the drawing, he smooths it out over the space on the table in front of me and starts pointing to each of us, though there's no question who is who in this picture. I'm the guy with all the muscles holding hands with Matty and my girl. There are cupcakes and hockey sticks and Legos. And I'm dead serious when I turn to him. "I love it. This is the best picture ever. Can I keep it?"

"Yes!" he bellows, his little hands coming up beside him. "I made it for you. I have one for me too and one for Mom."

At that, I glance up at Cammy, who gives me a shrug. "He's been busy."

Matty smiles down at his artwork. "This way you won't have to miss us so much when you're away for your games."

Before I can do more than open my mouth, he darts off, intent on showing me something else.

Cammy slides into the chair beside me and smiles down at the picture.

"He missed you. We have about seven versions of this picture around the house right now. I think he might have even given one to Jeremy."

Here we go. There's no way Cammy isn't going to tell me things have changed between them. She probably doesn't know that Matty spilled the beans about their sleepover—and the rational part of me knows it isn't actually any of my business anyway. But the idea that she wouldn't tell me they were together, giving it another try, bothers me almost as much as the idea of them actually together.

Which bothers me a lot. Even though it's not supposed to.

"I'm sure Jeremy loved that."

Cammy cocks her head, the soft huff of her laugh confirming he did not. "At least Matty drew him into the one he got."

I nod. Waiting.

"So tell me about your trip."

Or I guess, she's not.

Chapter 26

Cammy

here's nothing wrong with Jeremy's place. It's a comfortable two-bedroom walk-up in Wicker Park with plenty of light, a functional kitchen, and clean bathrooms. It's the kind of place I would have gotten for us if I didn't have a celebrity sister who'd insisted, first, that Matty and I live with her. And then, after she moved out and married Greg, that I stay.

So it's not the apartment, but every time I'm here I can't wait to leave. I don't like being in Jeremy's space. I don't like seeing the shelves filled with knickknacks from a life that didn't include Matty or me. It makes me resentful, and when I'm feeling as raw as I am about Rux—

"Cammy, you okay?" Jeremy asks, shoulder propped against the wall outside Matty's bedroom.

—I'm not sure I hide it as well as I'd like to.

"I'm fine," I choke out, checking my watch again and wondering what's keeping my kid. "Hey, Matty, you need some help packing up in there?"

Jeremy rubs the back of his neck and gives me an apologetic look. "Sorry, Cam. You're always so organized and have him packed up ready to go when I get him at your place. I should have had him ready to go. We were just... having a good time and I guess, selfishly, I didn't want to miss any of it by having him getting ready to go."

"Oh. Um, okay."

He clears his throat before meeting my eyes again. "Actually, I was kind of hoping we'd get a chance to talk anyway."

Talk?

Now that Jeremy has all my attention, I notice the way he's balling his hands in his jeans pockets and the sort of anxious vibe coming off him. My heart sinks.

"What is it?" Is he moving again? Leaving? Oh God, if he tells me that he's leaving our son again when he's only just become a part of his life. When Matty believed he was going to have an actual father—

"Cammy—" Jeremy takes a step closer, his hands coming up to my shoulders as he searches my eyes.

"Hey, look at me. Whatever you're thinking, stop. I'm asking if there's any chance that maybe once in a while I might be able to keep Matty for more than just an overnight. If maybe we could have the second day too or even a second night."

I shake my head, trying to clear the haze of panic enough to let the words filter through.

"No?" Jeremy asks, stricken.

"Oh, no. I mean, not no. I— I thought you were going to say something else and I—"

"You thought I was going to bail again." He says it without judgement but there's no mistaking the remorse in his eyes.

"I'm sorry, Jeremy."

He swallows. "Don't be. You have every reason to think that way. I've given it to you. And all I can do is keep on showing up and hope that with enough time you'll be able to start believing in me again. Trusting me."

I want to tell him I trust him already, but he's right. I don't. I'm waiting for the other shoe to drop, for him to realize life without a kid is more his speed. For some pretty distraction to step into his life and those priorities he swears by to change again.

He can see me wrestling with what to say and squeezes my shoulder. "In time, Cammy. I'm not going anywhere. In time, you'll see it. In time, I'll earn back your trust."

Taking a breath, I try to clear the moisture from my eyes. "Hey, Matty?"

"One second, Mom," he calls back as I swing the door to his room open.

"Honey, I have a zillion errands to run this afternoon. Would you like to come with me or… hang out here today and have your dad bring you home after dinner?"

THIRTY MINUTES later I'm parked in front of Rux's place.

Matty was beside himself, and Jeremy's gratitude unmistakable. I had nothing to worry about. My son's heart was fine. Jeremy wanted more of being a parent, not less. So why do I feel like I'm coming apart at the seams?

From the second I walked out of Jeremy's door, it was like I was on autopilot. All I wanted to do was talk to Rux. Tell him how my mind had automatically gone to Jeremy abandoning Matty again, how even finding out that quickly I'd been wrong, I'm so shaken I can hardly breathe. I want him to pull me into his arms for a hug. Even one of those half hugs would do, because what I need right now is to feel some of that unwavering strength around me.

But like a total chicken, I've been sitting downstairs worrying over whether I should go up. He ought to be home. Morning skate is over and the charity dinner he's attending isn't until seven. But as Rux pointed out, he has a lot going on. That psycho Waters keeps trashing him in one article after another, and the trade rumors are prevalent enough now to reach even me.

Would I just be *one more thing*, when he already has too much?

God, I wouldn't have even thought twice about going to him when I was upset before. And if I had, Rux would have reamed me out for being crazy. Because he was my guy. *My bestie.*

He said that wouldn't change. And yeah, things might have felt a little off in a way I couldn't quite pinpoint since last week, but maybe I needed to have a little more faith in the guy who's never let me down.

I'm halfway out of the car when I see him and, God, it's like I can breathe again. Like the world is right and it's only going to get better once he pulls me in to his side.

He's grinning, overlong hair blowing around in the wind as he holds the lobby door open. I raise my hand to wave, but stop halfway when a tall, slender brunette steps out. She's gorgeous. Beaming beside him. And before I can even try to talk myself into a scenario where she's just another tenant who happens to be leaving at the same time he is... she grabs his arm with both of hers and bounces as she starts walking beside him.

HER NAME IS DANIKA LENNOX. I didn't even have to wait a full day to find out who she was. Didn't have to go to Julia to find out either. All I needed to do was sit at the kitchen table and google Rux on my phone while my microwaved frozen entrée got cold.

The picture is less than an hour old, posted from the black-tie event Rux had told me about, but hadn't mentioned he'd be taking a date to.

Rux looks amazing in his custom tux, head angled toward hers, like he's listening intently to whatever she's saying. And Danika looks like a total bombshell. She's so put together with her perfect hair and makeup and dress... and a clutch so tiny, my phone wouldn't even fit in it let alone the rest of the crap from my huge mom purse.

Why wouldn't he have told me he had a date?

He would never want to hurt me. But maybe he didn't think it would... because it wouldn't matter to him. Because he's already moved on and that crazy possessive side of him just isn't engaged anymore.

My stomach turns and I push my untouched dinner aside.

God, I need to get over him. I need to put what we shared behind us… because we're friends. And just like we'd agreed would happen, that's all we are.

My phone pings with a text from Jeremy letting me know he and Matty are on their way up. I dump my dinner in the trash and wipe down the table. Head over to the front door just as Jeremy knocks.

The man is beyond dedicated to announcing his presence these days. Not that there's anything to interrupt.

I open the door and am rewarded with my own bit of sunshine when Matty gleefully throws his arms around me, thanking me for letting him stay longer. Then he's whizzing past me, mouth moving a mile a minute, as he tells me about making eggs with Jeremy and the park where they raced and then finally that he's going to take a shower and put all his things away on his own.

And then he's gone and Jeremy and I stand there in stunned silence for a few seconds before shaking our heads with a smile.

"Okay, maybe I shouldn't have given him the ice

cream after dinner." Walking past me, he holds up Matty's bag. "Can I drop this in his room?"

"That's great, thank you. And thanks for bringing him home."

I hear the shower turn on, accompanied by a series of thuds that make me wonder how one small boy can make so much noise.

Jeremy walks back out. "Least I could do."

He stuffs his hands into the pockets of his jeans and I can't help but notice how different he looks doing it from Rux. How it almost makes his shoulders look smaller instead of bigger.

Not that it matters.

"Cam, I really appreciate what you did for me today." He drops his head and lets out a long breath. "I appreciate every day. I know each one is a gift. That every time I get to see that boy smile or call me Dad, it's because of you."

"Jeremy—"

"Let me finish. Because, I've been wanting to say this for a while now and it never seems like the right time. But I need to get it out there."

"Okay. What do you want to say?"

"For seven years, you did it all. You were mother and father—everything our son needed to grow into the incredible kid he is now. I know you didn't get the breaks that come from having a second parent there with you every night. You didn't have the shoulder to cry on when you were overwhelmed. And you didn't have the one person who should have had your back through all the tough times. There's nothing I can do about the past, no way I can convey how sorry I am. How much I wish I'd done everything different, starting with the day I walked out on you."

Jeremy has talked about this before. And I appreciate the way he is taking ownership of his mistakes. But tonight it feels different. Like he's trying to tell me—

"Babe, I never should have left you." He steps into my space, eyes searching mine. "I've never stopped loving you."

No. I try to step back from what I should have seen coming, but the kiss catches me off guard. I freeze at the press of Jeremy's mouth against my own, a kiss I haven't had in more than seven years. One that's both foreign and familiar.

"*Jeremy*," I choke, trying to break the contact with a gentle push. But when my hands meet his chest, his covers mine and the noise he makes is pure misguided relief.

I pull away, shaking my head. "I'm sorry, Jeremy."

Chapter 27

Rux

The security in my building is top notch. No one gets in without approval. You can't even get security to call me if you aren't on a very short list.

Jeremy Levenson is on that list. So when he shows up at the front desk demanding to see me at the ass crack of dawn, they call up... And my world fucking ends because the only scenarios that involve this dickhead coming to my place are worst case.

The kind there's no coming back from.

Frantic, I trip getting out of bed, try to shake off the fog of sleep as I hop around, jerking on the first pants and T-shirt I can lay eyes on. I race out the front door, shoes in one hand, phone, wallet, and keys in the other.

What if it's Matty? Damn it, I can't breathe even thinking about it. His little body. That joyful face and staggering mind. His generous joyful heart.

I wish you were my dad.

I double over, bracing a hand on the wall as I try to breathe through the searing pain in my chest. If it was Matty, Cammy wouldn't leave him. But if it was Matty, and Cammy was okay... there's no chance in hell she wouldn't have called me herself.

It doesn't matter what's been going on between us. She would have called, because she would need me. More than Jeremy, more than even Julia—I'm the one she can count on. The one she turns to. No matter what. Forever. She knows it.

I know it. Christ, I feel like I've been back-checked into the boards.

Why the hell did I ever think walking away was the right choice? That giving them up was even fucking possible?

I can't lose them.

I can't. I love them.

I love them more than my own life. For once my eyes are open, and I'm praying for the chance to tell them. To beg Cammy for another chance to show her that I can be the man she deserves. That I want her in that white dress, smiling up at me. I want her today, tomorrow, and every moment of her forever.

They have to be okay. They have to. I would *know* if they weren't.

Where the hell is the elevator!

No missed calls or texts from Cammy, but my notifications are blowing up and I'm too terrified to open them.

Pull it together, man. Be ready.

I've got one shoe on by the time the elevator doors glide open and I get a look at Jeremy's ravaged expression.

They're going to be okay. Because they have to.

Hands limp at my sides, I stand. "Tell me."

Jeremy lurches forward and—

"*The fuck?* Did you just *punch* me?"

Based on the way he's furiously cradling his hand, looks like it. And then I'm smiling, my heart starting to beat again. Because this fucker isn't gutted... he's *pissed*. And I'm about to drop to my damn knees for that, but I don't want to risk Matty's dad doing something stupid like breaking his other hand trying to hurt me. Especially when I'm going to win my girl back, right out from under him.

"Dude, what's your issue?"

Jeremy sucks a breath, and stalks toward me. "*My issue?*" Clearly, I'm the only one who's feeling some relief. "My issue is that you're a goddamned hypocrite, Meyers. She's *in love with you!*"

The needle screeches off the vinyl and I blink.

"She's okay? Matty is okay?"

"What? Yeah, they're fine. Physically. But when they hear—"

That torn up spot in my chest starts to beat again. One thump. Two... two thousand.

"She *loves* me." All this time, I've been reminding myself there was a difference between love and being in love. Trying to wrestle my emotions back across the line to protect her and Matty. But I've been an idiot to think anyone could protect the two people I love most in the world better than I would. "Hey, Jeremy. Man, your hand doesn't look so good. Come in and I'll get you some ice."

He laughs, but the sound is bitter and again I see that shift between pain and rage and back again in his eyes.

"She told me last night. I thought with you two broken up and then you were out with that brunette—"

"Wait, what?" The brunette like the nutritionist Coach made half the guys on the team hire?

"—she'd be ready to give us another chance. I thought, deep down, she had to still love me the way I still love her. But she doesn't." He groans, his eyes shining. "Do you have any idea what it's going to do to her when she realizes that you lied to her? That you're every damn bit as bad as I am. *You're worse.*"

She doesn't love him.

She loves me.

He's clearly worked up. And there's something about what he's saying I know I should pay attention to, but—

"She hadn't seen the article yet," Jeremy snarls. "She doesn't know that she picked the one guy she and Matty should trust even less than me."

"What article?" All the hope and joy and relief that had started filling my chest evaporates, replaced with a sinking sense of dread. Jeremy isn't here swinging at me because he's jealous. He's here because he loves Cammy and whatever he read this morning was bad enough he was willing to take me on.

"Here you've been looking at me like the worst kind of asshole. Like you're so much better and you'd never let anyone down the way I did. Only that's not true, is it?"

Fuck. It's not possible. There's no way.

Beth said she didn't talk to Waters.

But even as I pull up my phone and open the first notification, I know someone did. The headline comes up.

"SLAYERS CAPTAIN RUXTON MEYERS

ABANDONED PREGNANT HIGH SCHOOL GIRLFRIEND… Leadership abilities in question."

Cammy

MY HANDS ARE SHAKING, my eyes a blur of tears and confusion.

It took everything I had to hold it together long enough for Natalie to come over and get Matty out of here. It's not even eight in the morning and the phone's been blowing up for an hour. One silent notification flashes across the screen after another. I can't turn it off in case something comes up with Matty.

And I can't stop watching the screen, waiting for the one call I need more than my next breath… Rux telling me that it's a lie. Because it has to be. I know it down to my soul, he wouldn't have done that. I know him… he would never have walked away like Jeremy did. Never.

He told me long ago that marriage and kids weren't in the cards for him. That he wasn't made of the stuff it took to be a good father or husband. But that doesn't mean—

The front door to the apartment bangs open and I

jerk around to see Rux rushing in, regret carved into every line of his face.

The dam inside me breaks and, holding out my phone, I choke on a sob. "Just tell me it isn't true. I know it already. *I do.* But I just need you to say it."

There's agony in his eyes and before he even opens his mouth, I want to call him a liar. Because it's not possible.

I know him.

Rux is the most loyal man I've ever met. The most ridiculously dedicated and faithful.

I love him.

"It's— Christ," he chokes out, raking a hand over his haggard face. Haunted eyes meet mine and I wait, leaning into the silence. "We weren't in high school."

And that's when it hits me. This is *the girl.* The one he was so torn up over after it ended. This is what nearly cost him his career. Regret on a Rux-level scale.

The air leaks from my lungs as I stumble toward the couch.

Rux is there beside me, taking my hands in his. Telling me he's sorry. He should have told me, but he was ashamed. All the while, I'm shaking my head, no. Thinking about those times I would see him staring at Matty with that strange mix of love, longing, and pain in his eyes.

I know him.

"Rux, make me understand," I beg, tears running down my face. "Tell me what happened. Because that article makes it sound like you got your high school girlfriend pregnant… and left." Left her to miscarry their baby alone. And never looked back.

Pressing a hand against my belly, I fight the rise of nausea.

I. Know. Him.

"I left, but not because of the baby. Not because I didn't want her."

"What?" I whisper, clutching at his forearms like I'm clutching at hope. "You didn't abandon her?"

"I might as well have. We were supposed to go to school together, but then at the last minute, I changed my mind and went to Juniors. She was so hurt. So mad. We'd had a plan, but I couldn't stick to it. I saw my shot and had to take it. I should have talked to her about it first, brought her with me, something. But I thought one of us should get to go to school. Maybe it would have been different if I did."

"She got pregnant?"

"Just before I got picked up in the draft. I found out when I surprised her at school." He swallows hard. Meets my eyes with a bleakness that devastates me. "She wasn't going to tell me. I begged her to keep the baby. We were supposed to get married. We'd planned it. I bought her a ring."

"Rux, why would she tell Waters you abandoned her?"

He looks past me. "She didn't. She called me a while ago. Let me know he'd been digging around. When she didn't give him anything, he must have found out about it from someone else."

"Did she lose the baby?" It's what the article said. But the way he said he begged her to keep it has me bracing for something else.

"She told me we could talk about it. But when I came back the next night she'd already terminated it. I —fuck, I know it's her choice, but I was wrecked. I asked her why she wouldn't wait for me. She was so angry." His head drops low. "She said I'd let her down too many times already. She'd seen what kind of man I was, only good for a good time. But I was unreliable, and the only thing she could count on was if she'd decided to keep the baby with me, she'd have two children to raise alone."

"Why would she say those things to you?" I gasp, breaking beneath the pure anguish in his words.

"She was angry. At herself. At me. It took a few years, eventually she sent me a letter. The baby wasn't mine. She felt like I'd abandoned her at school. Saw the posts on social from me hanging with guys outside of practice. It always looked like a party. And one night she drank too much and made a bad decision. Didn't know how to own up to it and it just got worse when I found out." His breath leaks out and he rubs his eyes with the heels of his hands. "If she'd told me, I would have forgiven her. I would have loved them both."

Oh God. "Rux, I'm so sorry."

"No." He turns to me. "Cammy, I'm the one who's sorry. I'm sorry you had to find out like this. That it scared you. That it hurt you."

"I wish you'd told me, but only because I hate that you've been carrying this alone all this time. I hate that there is any part of you blaming yourself." I hate that I suddenly understand those times that he joked about never getting married because he didn't want to have the kind of power to wreck someone's life like that. That when he leaned in and kissed my cheek telling me he'd rather be my bestie and keep me forever… I should have told him then and there that he would never let me down.

I reach for him, stroke his cheek.

His eyes close and then, because he really is the most perfect man, he pulls me into his lap and holds me against his chest. We stay like that for a long time, just holding each other. When his hand moves over my back, I sit up and—

"What are you wearing?"

Brows buckling, he looks down… and laughs.

I press my hand to his chest, and sigh. "There's my sunshine." Because that's what he is.

He shakes his head, gives me a crooked smile. "I was in kind of a rush this morning. Grabbed the first things I could get my hands on without thinking much about it."

And apparently the first things were his tuxedo pants and the T-shirt I got him to match the panties he'd gotten for me. It says, *I licked him so he's mine*, across the chest.

I run my fingers over those words, wishing they were true. Wishing this man was mine in all the ways a man could be.

I'm going to have to tell him I love him one of these days. I don't want any more secrets between us, and he can handle it. I know him.

Rux's big hand closes over mine.

My cheeks start to heat, and I realize what I was doing. That that reverent touch wasn't exactly on the right side of platonic. "Sorry."

"Don't be. I mean, it's true. You licked it and it's yours."

He doesn't mean it like I want him to.

He draws that trapped hand to the center of his chest, flattening it over his heart. "But this, pretty sure *this* has been yours far longer than that."

I blink. Feel those tears I'd barely gotten control of threatening a return.

He means in the way friends hold each other's hearts. Because we're besties.

Right?

I meet his eyes.

I know him. I trust him.

"I love you," I whisper, trusting that he knows me the same way.

The corner of his mouth hooks up and my belly does a little flutter. "Like *love*, love?"

My hand presses harder and I let him see all the things I've been trying to hide for these past weeks. "Like I've been dying without you, my heart breaking a little more every time I saw you and knew I needed to let you go."

"I wanted you to have more. I thought I couldn't give you the kind of confidence and security you deserved in your forever. But Cammy, I swear, I'm never going to stop working to become the man you deserve."

I shake my head. "Rux, do you *love*, love me?"

"So fucking much."

"Then you've already given me everything that matters, more than I ever dreamed of."

He swallows, opens his mouth. Closes it and looks away. But then looks back and it's there in his eyes.

The future neither of us ever believed we could have, the one we were too scared to see, but had been waiting for us all along.

"I love you, Cammy. I love Matty. And I'm going to ask you to marry me, but not yet."

I lean back and whisper, "What?"

"Yeah, don't want you to think it's just Rux being Rux, all rash and impulsive."

I shake my head. "But what if I love Rux being Rux, and rash and impulsive are a couple of my favorite things about you. Like loyal, loving, dedicated..."

God, that smile!

"Cammy?"

"Rux."

"I'm going to ask you, but not until after Matty knows we're *together*, together. Give him a chance to get used to seeing us as a couple before throwing a wedding at him."

I love this man with my whole heart and soul.

"Good plan," I say, shifting in his lap so my legs straddle his. "But if you're not going to ask me to marry you right now... what are you going to do?"

He groans, pulling me against him with one hand at my hip and the other behind my neck. "I'm going to love you." Our mouths meet in a kiss that's so sweet and right, and hot and perfect, I shiver with the realization forever is already here.

An hour later, we're still on the couch, now a tangle of bare limbs, damp skin, and endless kisses. Rux mutters a curse against my neck and lifts his head.

"Uh, Sunshine, I didn't mention it earlier… but umm… we should probably check on Jeremy."

My brow lifts. "Why?"

Rux cringes. "Okay this is going to sound bad, but I'm pretty sure my face accidentally broke his hand."

Rux

"BUT *WHY* WON'T you tell me what happened?" Matty whines, running his little fingers over the cast on his dad's hand.

I feel Cammy tense up against my side, where we're curled up on the couch in her place.

A week later, things have settled down. Beth came out with a statement debunking the article Waters posted while preserving both of our privacy as much as possible. When I was worried about rushing things with Matty after he'd seen his parents napping together—Cammy thankfully debunked that misunderstanding about the nap that wasn't actually together. And I debunked the business with the nutritionist who I already let go. Unfortunately the trade rumors proved true, only they weren't about me.

Matty saw me kiss his mom goodbye a few nights ago—closed mouth, no tongue, thank you—and spent the next two days giving me the kind of face-splitting grins where I could count all his teeth. Safe to say my man is on board, but I still want to give him a little time.

Not too much though.

And as for Jeremy… he shakes his head from where he's crouching beside Matty. "I'm not proud of what I did, but I'm going to be honest with you so you feel like you're able to be honest with me… I hit Rux."

"What!" Matty shrieks, his head spindling between all of us, horror in his blue eyes.

"It was a mistake, and Jeremy and I made up," I add quickly.

"It was a mistake." Jeremy nods. "I believed something that wasn't true, and I acted before I thought."

Eyes as wide as saucers, Matty whispers, "What did you think he'd done?"

"Something to hurt your mom's feelings. But I was wrong."

Matty looks to me. "Did he knock you out?"

Beside me, Cammy quakes with restrained laughter but she gets it under control.

I can see the awe in his little eyes and instead of telling him the truth—his dad punches like a pussy—I say, "Really close."

Jeremy clears his throat. "Thing is. Rux was the bigger man that day, Matty." He puts his hand over his chest. "In here. He could have hit me back. Pounded me into next year. But even though I hit him when he wasn't expecting it, and he had every right to retaliate... he cared more about you and your mom than getting even."

And damn, that's some pretty big man shit right there. Cammy seems to notice, because she gives my hand a squeeze.

I clear my throat. "Matty, we were both thinking about you guys that day. Because we both love you."

He nods and looks at his mom with earnest eyes. "We're lucky like that."

Cammy ruffles his hair, then looks to me. "We're the luckiest."

I couldn't agree more.

Rux

Three years later

"*A*ww, come on. With the eyes?" Jesus, one look at those beautiful blues and I feel myself cracking. Which would be a mistake. I'm sure of it.

Any other time, I'd have my girl backing me up. Being sensible. Suggesting we stop, take a breath, and think things through.

But surprise... Pregnant Cammy is an *impulsive Cammy*. It's fucking adorable, and about 95% of the time I'm in full support.

She wants tacos at three in the morning? I'll drive.

A boat because being on the water is so relaxing? We're cruising out of Belmont Harbor by noon.

But this?

"Sunshine, we spent months talking about getting a dog." Weighing the pros and cons. Debating over a male or female. If we wanted a puppy. When the best time to bring it into the house would be. "We have a plan." Hell, we spent more time nailing it down than we did on the details for our Fiji wedding and that was phenomenal.

She blinks up at me, smiling as she snuggles a wriggling, licking, silky puppy that's all eyes, ears and feet… and *not* the dog we drove out to this foster house to pick up. "I know, I know. We did… *But they're brothers.*"

Oh no. I can't resist that smile. And when the next flurry of licks scores her bubbly laugh—I start to panic.

Three years in and you'd think I'd have developed some tolerance to my wife's laugh, but I'm as gone for her as I was the day we said I do. Hell, from the day we met. I might not have been ready to see the Happily Ever After on the wall back then, but from the start, this woman has been everything.

And I don't want to let her down when sixth month hormones have her acting a little… *rash*.

I turn to Matty—shit, we're supposed to call him *Matt* now—for support, except I don't know what I'm thinking, because he's ten and giving me the same big eyes his mother is while the puppy we came for covers his face with kisses. "Please, Rux? The house is plenty big for two."

It's big enough for a hell of a lot more than that. We bought the place a year and a half ago when we decided we were ready to start trying for a baby, hoping when it's all said and done we'll be a family of five.

But no matter whether we have the space for a second dog or not, this is a decision we'll be living with for years.

The puppy in Cammy's arms gives up a hoarse little bark and my chin pulls back.

What the—?

Matt's eyes bug. "No way."

Cammy's jaw drops. Then, grinning like a kid on Christmas morning, she holds up the puppy, looking from it to me and back. "Did you say, 'Rux?'"

"No, he didn't," I snap, just as Matt giggles, "Yes, he did!"

The panic is real. Because now I'm not just up against my gorgeous wife and amazing kid... that fucking puppy is working me too.

Cammy tucks the puppy into her arm and I help her up. Her hand moves to her belly and for a second all I can think about is this morning when I kissed every inch of it and then lower until her breathy moans filled our room.

"Babe," she says all soft and sweet. "Maybe you should hold him for a second."

I know better. I do. But I reach for him anyway, taking that warm body in my hands.

I tell myself I'm a badass hockey stud and I don't get soft for puppies. But then those little paws are hanging over my thumbs and his tiny tail is wagging so hard his whole body shakes.

I want to do the right thing. I want to be *reasonable*, not *rash*.

He lets out another throaty bark that sounds freakishly close to my name and looks up at me with the big eyes that beg me to take him home too.

Damn.

"What are you thinking?" Cammy asks.

"Sunshine, I'm thinking I love you."

I'm thinking about that night with the tacos, and how the only thing better than seeing Cammy dancing outside that taco truck when she took her first bite was when we got home later... and she let me use Bob on her. I'm thinking about how much fun we have on that boat. And I'm thinking about that very first kiss at the Five Hole, and how sometimes those rash decisions from our past give us a future better than we ever imagined.

She gives me the smile I'll never get enough of.

The one that makes Matt groan and roll his eyes. "I love you too."

I pull her in for a hug. "So what do you say we bring these little guys home?"

Thank you for reading DIRTY REBOUND! I hope you had as much fun with Rux & Cammy as I did. Hungry for more Slayers Hockey?

DIRTY TALKER is next! Pre-Order Wade & Harlow's story here: http://www.books2read.com/Dirtytalkermlk

If you loved DIRTY REBOUND please consider leaving a review.

Also by Mira Lyn Kelly

SLAYERS HOCKEY

DIRTY SECRET (Vaughn & Natalie)

DIRTY HOOKUP (Quinn & George)

DIRTY REBOUND (Rux & Cammy)

DIRTY TALKER (Wade & Harlow - Coming 2021)

BACK TO YOU

HARD CRUSH (Hank & Abby)

DIRTY PLAYER (Greg & Julia)

DIRTY BAD BOY (Jack & Laurel)

DARE TO LOVE

TRUTH OR DARE (Molly & Ty)

TOUCH & GO (Ava & Sam)

NOW & THEN (Brynn & Ford)

COMING AROUND AGAIN (McTark Re-releases)

Just Friends (Matt & Nikki)

All In (Lanie & Jason) - coming soon

THE WEDDING DATES

MAY THE BEST MAN WIN (Jase & Emily)

THE WEDDING DATE BARGAIN (Max & Sarah)

JUST THIS ONCE (Sean & Molly)

DECOY DATE (Brody & Gwen)

WAKING UP

WAKING UP MARRIED (Megan & Connor)

WAKING UP PREGNANT (Darcy & Jeff)

UNCONNECTED NOVELS

ONCE IS NEVER ENOUGH (Nichole & Garrett)

NEVER STAY PAST MIDNIGHT (Levi & Elise)

THE S BEFORE EX (Ryan & Claire)

FRONT PAGE AFFAIR (Payton & Nate)

WILD FLING OR A WEDDING RING (Cali & Jake)

Acknowledgments

Fun fact: There's more to creating a book than just writing the words. A lot more!

The magic that goes into each book that finds it's way onto your eReader or shelf extends from that first willing ear to beyond the last set of eyes checking for typos. And I am beyond grateful for every single one of the people continually proving that writing is a team sport.

So huge thanks to Lexi Ryan, Lisa Kuhne, Jennifer Haymore, Kara Hildebrand, Sandra Shipman, Karin Enders, Crystal Perkins, Lori Rattay, Jessica Alcazar, Annika Martin, Zoe York, Skye Warren, Najla Qamber Designs, Wander Book Club, Tara Carberry and Nicole Resciniti. To all the girls from Write All The Words, the PJ Party, my Promo team and Eagle Eyes, and the reviewers and bloggers who help me spread the word about my books. To my family who puts up with my crazy hours and pig pen office and my friends who are the best break from deadline crazy.

And especially to you! Thank you for reading.

((HUGS)) Mira

About the Author

Hard core romantic, stress baker, and housekeeper non-extraordinaire, Mira Lyn Kelly is the USA TODAY bestselling author of more than a dozen sizzly love stories with over a million readers worldwide. Growing up in the Chicago area, she earned her degree in Fine Arts from Loyola University and met the love of her life while studying abroad in Rome, Italy… only to discover he'd been living right around the corner from her back home. Having spent her twenties working and playing in the Windy City, she's now settled with her husband in Minnesota, where their four amazing children and two ridiculous dogs provide an excess of action and entertainment. www.miralynkelly.com

Looking to stay in touch and keep up with my new releases, sales and giveaways?? Join my newsletter at miralynkelly.com/newsletter and my Facebook reader group at MiraLynKellyPJParty. We'd love to have you!!